High Spirits

Short Stories on Dominican Diaspora

High Spirits

Short Stories on Dominican Diaspora

* ★ *

Camille Gomera-Tavarez

LQ

LEVINE QUERIDO

Montclair | Amsterdam | Hoboken

This is an Arthur A. Levine book

Published by Levine Querido

www.levinequerido.com • info@levinequerido.com

Levine Querido is distributed by Chronicle Books, LLC

Library of Congress Control Number: 2021943709

ISBN: 978-1-64614-129-6

FSC
www.fsc.org

MIX
Paper from
responsible sources
FSC™ C144853

Printed and bound in China

Published April 2022

First Printing

To La Familia Gomera
y La Familia Tavarez
whose stories inspire me
in everything I do.
Bendiciones y muchísimo amor.

Legend:

~~~ X ~~~ divorce
~~~~~~ marriage
———— children
– – – – adoption

Family tree:

CRISTOBAL JIMENEZ ~~~ CONSUELA

- NORENA ~~~ RAFAEL
  - (5 brothers)
  - FRANKLYN
- EUGENIO (6 wives)
- LUPE + RAUL ~~~ MARK
  - MARITZA
  - ALBERTO (TITO) + LUCIANA
    - JORGE

JOSÉ BELÉN ～～～ LA DOÑA

MABEL ～～～～ JOSÉ II

JOSÉ III

MARA ～

ARIBEL

DAYANERA

YOLANDA

CHRISTIAN

RITA
(PR)

GIANCARLOS

GABRIEL

EVELYN

LAURA ～

CRISTABEL

JOSÉ IV

EMELY

ANA

HENNESSY

YOANSON

I.
Stickball

*I*t had been happening more and more lately. The pulls. It was well beyond Gabriel's capabilities to figure out their motivations or underlying meanings. His specialty was philosophy, not psychology. Besides, maybe they were harmless. Walking up the marble steps of the Social Sciences building, a sprightly young student intersected his path. She aimed a neon flyer at him, spouting about some event or other. He accepted the sheet hastily and continued deeper into his pool of thought.

After the last incident, he'd wondered if maybe it was due time to consider some form of therapy. That was only a half joke, obviously. As an academic, he felt a grain of shame that his family's antiquated beliefs on mental health still made compelling arguments within him. But he couldn't very much help it. Gabriel's parents would probably disown him if it ever got back to the island that he had succumbed to the scam of paying someone to listen to his problems. That was for rich Americans and murderers. "You talk to us. That's what family is for, mijo," he could hear his father's whiskey and cigar-stained voice now. "Who could know you better than us?"

Because, you see, Gabriel's family knew absolutely everything about the carefully constructed persona he'd spent his adult life presenting to them. He'd pieced it together with the caring, gentle hands of the piñata sculptor he would pass on the way to his grandmother's house as a boy. Each slice of wet newspaper a little bit of the truth, hardening into a fragile shell over time.

He paused, meeting with the door of his classroom and the long-hidden memory of the piñata he'd cracked at his fifth birthday celebration. Before yesterday, really, all the other pulls had been pleasant. He'd almost wished to remain in the past, with the salt of the ocean and ripening mangoes in the Atlantic wind. Sometimes Gabriel believed things were better then, despite his numerous counter-arguments that "nostalgia was a sign of human ineptitude" which he vocalized among his peers after a few glasses of Chardonnay. The foolishness of dwelling in his own past was evident to him. Still, the pulls made it all seem so real. The sense of present-day reality, shredded away into an innocent world free of any dense philosophical conundrums.

The last time it happened, he was standing in a queue for lunch. His first day teaching at the college. As he approached the tub of buffet-style black beans, he found himself being pulled closer by the wistful aroma. Strange, as he'd detested the sight of cooked beans since the moment his family had pooled their resources to send him to study in the land of burgers and pizza at age twenty. Soon he was standing in front of them, his eyes misplaced somewhere among the shimmering black mounds before him.

Gabriel stared into the food until his mother slapped his wrists with her wooden spoon and commanded him to fight the devil living within his eyes. The child jerked with a start, taking a large, uneven breath of the evening palm leaves into his lungs. Doña Mabel assessed her son's condition quickly and then turned back to stirring her pot. She was accustomed to his wild stares. By now, she caught them early and snapped him out of it with expert precision, as advised by Señor Leon, the town priest. Anyone could see that when the boy was in a state, it was as if his soul was possessed by multiple devils. Doña Mabel prayed every night and graciously accepted the bombardment of recommendations on this miracle oil or that miracle herb she encountered every Sunday, though she knew with as much certainty she held in the sun rising the next morning that her son would be just fine. With time.

Gabriel took the plates and silverware in his chubby arms. He steadied his balance and went to set the table. He could hear the cries of his older brothers in the yard.

"Higher! Throw it higher!"

Their shrieks pierced through the sounds of the street and the clatter within the kitchen. Gabriel could see them in blurred streaks passing through the door-shaped hole in the back of the house. His desire to join his brothers tricked his eyes into revealing a softness he could never quite hide. He finished setting the table and approached his mother with his weapon of innocence at the ready.

Doña Mabel tilted her head towards the yard. Gabriel attempted to hide his excitement and ran to join his brothers. Christian and Josélito paid no attention to their little brother and continued with their game of stickball. The sock they used as a ball was already green and brown and smelled worse than the feet that had once worn it. It had endured being whipped by tree branches and slammed into walls for months now. Christian had started stuffing rocks into it when it had begun to deflate. Soon it would be lost in a ditch somewhere among the palm trees and a new sock would step up to replace it. But for now, it remained the primary source of entertainment for the Belén boys.

The wooden front door slammed to indicate the arrival of their father. The door always slammed, held together shabbily with nails and repurposed hinges. But everyone tensed when that particular slam echoed through the house. José Sr once said that he would slam every door in the house as hard as he wanted, since he'd been the one whose hands had built it. The sun had not yet set, so it was unusual for him to be home, but neither the boys nor Doña Mabel paid any mind. His boots made their way through the house, spreading dirt as they went. "Hola, amor. Everything alright?" posed La Doña from beneath a steaming pot of rice. José Sr. let out a curt grunt and sank into his brown leather sofa chair which outlined his memory in a dark brown tint.

Gabriel watched patiently from his seat in a patch of dry dirt as the sock ball moved between his brothers. He was content in his observation, imagining how one day he might be a famous pelotero for one of the national teams. He'd never thrown a sock ball in his life, but he was sure that he could if he really tried. Josélito didn't make it seem hard. He ran with ease, without panting or coughing.

From the kitchen, a ceramic dish collided with the ground. The boys and the birds all froze for a microsecond, looking towards the minor explosion, before they resumed their activities. The shuffling of feet indicated all was well.

Gabriel then felt compelled to get up and watch from the other side of the yard, where he could see Christian

hitting the sock ball more clearly. He scurried around
his brothers so as not to get hit. His feet bounced lightly
along the dirt and patches of grass, gracefully avoiding
shattered glass or bottle caps. He stared downward as his
bare toes crossed one in front of the other, in front of the
other, in front of the other. The rhythm soothed him and
drowned out all other sounds. Only a faint pulse within
him remained to complement the soothing rhythm of one,
two, one, two, one . . .

A robust womanly shriek broke the silence and
pushed a handful of swallows to escape into the purple
sky. Gabriel's rhythm stopped. He looked up, surprised
and unfamiliar with his surroundings. The dirt under
his feet was soggier now, and dark. Something rustled
ahead of him in the sea of cattails reflecting the sunset
off their feathery tufts. Gabriel's knees gave in and he
crashed against a rock jutting out amongst the damp
soil. His heart sped up slightly and his lungs attempted to
keep up. The sky was suddenly a sickly pink eternity, alien
and overwhelming. He must have walked at least two
miles without even realizing it. The boy was wholly alone,
isolated from everything he knew. He was not scared, he

affirmed. Papa José would tell him not to be scared. He raised himself, turned one hundred and eighty degrees, and started up his rhythm again. His faith and his legs would take him home. This was his only option.

Eventually, the clay Spanish roof tiles and patched-up wooden door he'd prayed for came into view. Gabriel allowed himself to run now. Past the baker, the tire shop, the house of Señora Imogen who made piñatas. The door closed behind him with a timid slam. He hoped to be spared a spanking. Or worse — a high-volume lecture. Perhaps his brothers would be blamed since it was they who had been the negligent caretakers. Maybe his mother would even let Gabriel choose the stick for their punishment. This gave him the courage to step further into the room.

Papa's chair was empty. Chants of "Higher! Higher!" persisted in the yard like a film frozen in time. Doña Mabel was stationed in an old blue kitchen chair, wrapping her right hand in fabric as red liquid swam through the seams. She seemed not to notice him. The table was still set, now adorned with a fresh pot of rice and bowl of shredded pork. Gabriel looked from the sofa chair to his mother and then to the cut on his ash-ridden knee. He quickly wiped his knee with the back of his hand. And ran for the door-shaped hole past the kitchen.

"And where were you?" Mabel's brow furrowed briefly as Gabriel attempted to get past her. She plucked the child's arm from beneath her with her free hand. Her expression continued her question, unrelenting. Gabriel stuttered that he had been fetching the ball for his brothers as he tugged his arm slightly in the direction of the yard, wishing to be freed. "Hmmm . . ." She interrogated him without speaking. He knew that she knew he was lying. She let him go.

"Boys! Christian! Junior! The table!"

The house filled with laughter and youth as the two came filing in. Mabel calmly instructed Gabriel to go get the habichuelas from the sink. As Gabriel nervously obeyed, she readied to set her wrath upon her older sons. "Where's Papa?" one of them asked. She motioned to Gabriel. "Why is he bleeding? What did you do? You couldn't get the ball yourselves? Goddammit none of you ever show a drop of care for each other! If you would only pay attention at church, I swear . . ." The protesting began. "WHAT? We didn't do anything!" "He's lying! He always lies!"

Christian turned to pounce on his youngest brother. He had the look of an adopted alley cat who had finally discovered the hole in which the house mouse lived. Gabriel watched as Christian's eyes turned into a glazed black pool. His hearing shut down, but not before registering the familiar sound of ceramic breaking on the floor. A stream of black beans soaked his toes, or at least he thought they did. The solid dirt floor turned to swamp. His mother and brothers were gone. All that remained was black. He felt like he was swimming through black with his arms propelling him, turning with the same rhythm as his legs. One, two. The leather sofa chair walked up to him, larger than the ceiling which had disappeared as well. The naked stars above shot downward like laser beams, repelling him deeper into the earth. The sofa chair leapt toward him. Gabriel struggled to grasp for something, anything. Teeth broke through the leather shell and released a wave of rotting, yellowed stuffing.

An army of campus safety guards held down Gabriel's body as he spasmed on the checkered cafeteria floor. He kicked them, wailing, with his back arched away from the ground. He awoke when the paramedics arrived, so capable in all manners now that they merely performed a quick physical before allowing him to carry on with his day (as he so vehemently wished). By then he was no longer hungry. He quickly collected his things. Gabriel watched as his crime scene of spattered black beans was swept away into nothing by a janitor's mop.

II.
Colmado

The pale blue paint on the house exterior had deeper cracks than her abuelo's toasted hands, its hue fading faster than his fleeting mind. Cristabel's cousins on the island would recount when they were all grown how despite his worsening dementia, the old man would still get up at the same time every morning, with the sun and the roosters, and open his little blue store just as he had done even before her own father was a young teen. Probably even before there were cars or telephones or any signs of modern life. The actual age of Abuelo's colmado was ultimately unknown. As surrounding colmados came and went in the town of Hidalpa, her abuelo's store had persevered long enough to become a local staple.

Despite pressures to adopt her father's town as her own, Cristabel had never been able to shake the American city she'd known for most of her life. The languidness of the days in Hidalpa weighed on her as densely as its humid summer air. She often tried to combat the New Yorker within who desired fast walking and trains to catch, but it was a losing fight. Hidalpa was a history she'd inherited, but it was not her own. Still, two months after her abuela died suddenly, Cristabel paid a visit to her abuelo to check on his condition. It had been five years since her last brief visit, and it looked the same way it had since the 1950s. To her surprise, her cousins had not exaggerated in their calls. All the old man could talk about was his colmado. He asked about his orders and his books and his accounts. Occasionally, he asked about his dear wife, where was she? And one uncle or cousin would lie that she'd gone to the city for some medicine and that she'd be back soon. And he'd instantly accept this feasible story. Then his mind was back to his colmado in the next beat. That was how most of the visit went.

The one thing that stuck in Cristabel's mind when she was sitting on the plane heading back home from Hidalpa was an article she'd read in *The New Yorker*. It was all about how marriage was good for men and bad for women — a man's lifespan extended if he were married to a woman and a woman's decreased. Without the presence of Cristabel's abuela, she'd noticed the house had turned still and careful. Everything was fake, a stage. Her abuelo was like a sick child who'd been tricked into believing they were king of the castle. He needed to open the store the same time every day, have his café con leche ready for him at the table, eat the same supper while sitting at the head of the table, and drink a forty-ounce beer until he slept in his leather chair. Only one or two relatives were ever there at a time, playing their parts in this reenactment of life in the old house.

* * *

When the old house was still in its golden era and her abuela was still alive, every Christmas vacation Crista's sisters, father, uncles, aunt and all twenty of her cousins would crowd the house that her abuelo had built of aluminum siding and wood and dirt. They were constantly sleeping stacked on top of each other, eating over one another, and waiting for hours to use one of the two explicitly gendered outhouses. With the overwhelming number of female cousins, the outhouse rules were bent each morning. One had to wake up at the crack of dawn to get a chance at a decent morning shower. Sometimes the younger children took their freezing cold showers in pairs, just to save time and water.

Crista, at the time, was a quiet but happy child. "Is she mute?" her uncles would ask her father. "Ella solo dice 'sí' o 'no'." Of course, she understood more than that, she just never knew what to say around grown- ups. Her days were spent running around the peaceful streets swatting sticks at other children and returning home for endless amounts of white-cold glass soda bottles from the colmado's back fridge. This winter month in the island heat was the only time her father allowed her to drink soda with all her meals. Each day she tried new flavors: grape, strawberry, orange, apple, ginger; even the Sprite and Coca-Cola tasted better. She could never figure out as a child why the sodas in Dominican Republic tasted better than any other soda she'd ever had. When she grew older she realized the secret ingredient — real cane sugar from the fields, with a deep sweetness as refreshing as mint.

One winter, when Crista was about ten years of age, she sat in the living room contently reading Roald Dahl's *Matilda* to the puzzlement of her horde of female cousins, who had gone out to the baseball park to watch the local boys practice. Crista didn't like the baseball park so much. The steel bleachers were unbearably hot and the older boys would often make fun of them, mostly of her and her weird American accent. Before she'd entered the park she had seldom been aware that she possessed an accent. She had just turned a fresh page of her book when her abuelo emerged from his bedroom and asked her, in his thick country accent, if she could man the colmado for him.

He wore a childlike grin, begging her to indulge him in this transparent attempt at connecting with his American granddaughter. She felt her adolescent nerves bubbling up slightly at the possibility of social interaction which this invitation suggested, but she closed her book and followed behind him and his worn linen trousers anyways. Abuelo's colmado was attached to the side of the house, with the back entrance of the store running right through the old couple's tiny bedroom, behind vanity mirrors stained with browning photographs and draped mosquito nets and drying bedsheets. She kept following him through the dimly lit room. As he lifted the final hanging bedsheet that served as the barrier between house and work, Crista's eyes discovered a new perspective on the family store.

"Traje a tu nieta para que te acompañe, mi negra," he spoke to his wife, who sat behind the cash register, holding a worn notebook and pencil. Her abuela's eyes lit up at the sight of the girl. They were cloudy behind her thick glasses. Her gnarled hands brought Crista's ten-year-old cheek to her lips and motioned towards the wooden chair beside her own. She was sitting in that chair like it had taken her a long time to get in it, and it would take her a long time to get out.

Crista's abuelo smiled profusely, exchanging his gaze between the two. Crista wondered what task he felt he had achieved to be glowing with so much pride.

"Vengo ahora." And then he disappeared behind the bedsheet, without waiting for a response.

The elderly woman inched her glasses higher up her nose with the back of her wrinkled thumb and returned to the complex accounting work she seemed to be doing.

"Siéntate, niña." Crista finally took a seat beside her. It always seemed so important to her grandparents that Crista and the other children be seated. She was a girl who didn't talk much and her abuela knew this. They sat in silence amongst the buzzing of the store. Crista telepathically thanked her abuela for not pressing her with cordial questions. The temperature was too high that morning for cordial questions. A dusty fan spun above them on the ceiling.

Taking a look around her, Crista realized she'd never really known how much the colmado had to offer. Two men in the front of the store were drinking beer by a tall table and listening to the radio. There were plantains, bananas, ropes of garlic, and onions hanging from the ceiling above, ripe for plucking at the request of a customer. The glass counter before her contained a rainbow array of fruit-flavored candies. Crista did her best to suppress the urge to slip a tamarind chew in her pocket. And even knowing the back fridge was at her disposal, she found it hard to resist the pull of the bright soda fridge in front.

Just as Crista was hoping she wouldn't actually have to do any work, a man wearing a sleeveless shirt entered the store in quick strides.

He looked to the small, nervous girl behind the counter and asked, "¿A cómo son los plátanos?"

Crista momentarily froze in the shock that she could be mistaken for someone who knew the answer. Before she could panic, her abuela, still looking down as she counted coins between her wrinkled hands, whispered, "Dile que son a cinco pesos."

Without even giving it a second thought, Crista replied to the man in Spanish, plucked the fruit from above her, handed him his plátanos, took his twenty-five pesos, handed back two ten peso coins, and bid farewell with a cheerful "¡Gracias!" A successful transaction. He disappeared as quickly as he entered.

Crista's heart was pounding. His face had not given any indication she had revealed herself as an American. Was it natural instinct? The accent and mannerisms of her ancestors finally kicking in? She was just about to present a proud smile to her abuela when she heard the crashing of coins on the ground. Her abuela sat with her hands laid out for half a second before giving a little chuckle at her own silliness. She glanced up at her granddaughter, above the rim of her glasses, and Crista could see a spark of youthfulness beneath her cloudy hazel eyes. A moment more of the coins remaining on the ground between them almost caused Crista to let out a laugh herself.

But then her abuelo suddenly appeared from behind the bedsheet again, like a flash of lightning before the torrential rains that sometimes overtook the town of Hidalpa. A fast anger was behind his eyes. The change in emotions was so abrupt it made Crista fall back in her chair. He asked what had happened? Can't he leave the store alone with her for two minutes? Is she really getting this old? No, no, no, she can't get away with this. Ridiculous. And in front of the girl?

Crista stared, wondering if she should intervene, knowing her limitations as a child — even worse, as a girl. She had never feared her abuelo before. He demanded his wife get down on the ground and pick up the coins. His accusing finger forcefully prompted her to action. At this, Crista finally attempted to bend to pick them up herself, but she was met with her abuelo's hand on her chest.

"No, déjala."

Crista said nothing, but her eyes made their own lasting judgments. Memory would warp her impression of this moment when it returned to her at age twenty-five on a plane back to New York City. But the picture of her abuelo giving this command would remain unfaded.

She watched, in pain, as the woman slowly hiked up her thin house dress and bent her old, swollen knees before her rigid husband. Crista looked tensely between the two. Her abuela looked up at her granddaughter briefly, as she collected the coins in her palms. Sweat was building on the her face. Her glasses were slipping away from her button nose. Then, the most curious smirk curled on the edge of her lips. All at once, she was saying, "I'm sorry, dear," and, "He is an old fool, isn't he?" It was as if the punchline to a sad inside joke had been delivered, and Crista, in the way children do, understood something in what she did not understand.

She did not return her abuela's smile. She did not feel like laughing.

* * *

At the baggage claim of JFK Terminal 5, Cristabel wondered why she had never told her father about her morning working at the colmado as a child. She had left him now on the other side, working his shift as his father's nurse. She remembered contemplating telling him that very same afternoon over supper when she was ten years old. It was as she had been passing him the plate of cut avocados that she decided not to. The way he smiled gingerly at the swells in her abuela's feet and helped her set his father's place at the head of the table. His aged face growing identical to his mother's with time as he played her part now in the staged reenactment of the old house. Cristabel realized her father must have already known then her abuela's inside jokes. He had learned to laugh. She wondered if, one day, far off into the distance of a classic Hidalpan sunset, she would ever find herself in on the joke.

III.
Swimming in Circles

*B*y now, the teenagers had begun throwing flaming bottles of Presidente along the perimeter of El Parque Central. Apart from these little fires, it was the kind of pitch black outside that made you sure you were in the middle of nowhere. In Hidalpa, El Parque was like a carousel of sins on Año Nuevo. There was a certain magic pulling the town in circles as half the town engaged in a promenade around the park. It was as if with each step, they collectively wound up a giant clock, gaining enough power to propel themselves into another journey around the sun.

Josélito — now José by his own declaration and

sometimes "Chito" by a stubborn mother — could hardly differentiate between the outside warmth and the warmth brewing within his teenage belly. Every smashed bottle and firework brought on another frantic tug from his younger brother, Gabriel. He was the type of child that always seemed to be in the way.

"Diablo, Gabby, calm down. You wanna go home, little man? We can go home then, damn it!"

Gabriel's bright white eyes shook "no."

"Alright, then. Stop being a baby."

Their mother had let Gabriel out of her clutches this New Year's Eve. The clock struck twelve, the grapes were eaten, the bendiciones were said, and the town erupted in musical explosion. Even the roosters were heard joining in celebration of another year's existence. While the roosters were free to roam and find their hens, José was chained to his brother before he had the chance to escape. Somehow, the middle brother, Christian, had been able to flee to the neighbor's house during the bendiciones. José had scarcely ever thought Christian to be smart until then.

"Por favor, do three rounds with him and bring him home, Chito," his mother had begged on Gabriel's behalf.

A stern nod from his father, his namesake, sealed José's fate. "And don't bring him around your heathen friends con sus tira pops y vaina con fuego esos cracking bottles. If he loses an eye like el niño del lado, you better find somewhere else to sleep."

"Gimme two or three pesos to get him un helado then?"

José kept the money rolled in his sock now, as they approached their second procession around the park. He had the thin gold chain he'd gotten for his birthday draped around his neck. He wore his best linen church shirt, and the leather belt he'd cleaned and greased that morning. He waved around his secret brew of rum and mabí (now half empty) every time he saw someone he recognized. José's friends all sat on park benches with girls on their laps and seemingly no worries or burdens. Yet here José was. Shackled.

He looked down at Gabriel, who marveled at the sights around him like a tourist.

For a second time now, they passed Señora Milagros and her daughter Estervina at the fritura stand, wafting the smell of fried goods through the chaos. José watched Estervina step out and kick away a stray mini firecracker with a red heel, revealing her bare leg. He decided then that the three pesos had her name on them and set his eyes on the liquor store attached to the back of Don Luis's truck, up ahead. He put the brakes on their procession.

"Go play with your friends, Gabby, I'll be right back." José motioned towards the toddlers playing in the central stone gazebo, surrounded by adolescent mothers. Gabriel stared up at his brother with an annoyed, sunken look in his eyes.

"Ha. Ha."

"Oh? Who's laughing?" José raised his brows and shooed Gabriel away. He proceeded ahead, calling out for a rum and Coke.

* * *

He turned to face the procession counterclockwise now, with a target on Milagros' fritura stand. A second stereo had turned up, blasting raunchy bachata mixtapes against the already blasting Fernando Villalona that someone's uncle was playing on a turntable. The crowd adjusted the volume of their shouting conversations accordingly.

The sound was deafening, but somehow comforting as it overpowered the nervous rhythms within him.

Estervina.

"José! ¿Que lo qué, montro?"

        "¡Ey, Berto! Todo bien, what's good?"

Estervina. He kept walking.

"José!"

        "Marco! Be careful, brother!"

Estervina.

"¡El Belén!"

        "¡Ya tu sabes!"

Estervina.

"Yes?"

José stared at the brown-skinned girl in front of him, with waves of jet-black hair shimmering as she handed a hot, fresh-fried quipe to the child beside him. He slathered on the slickest smile he had and offered her mother the glass of rum and coke.

"Aren't you looking something lovely this Año Nuevo, Señora Milagros? Any chance you might let your daughter step out?"

Señora Milagros sent a half-amused look to her daughter.

"It's fine, Mami. I can st—"

"Ah, vete, before I change my mind. Don't bring back any babies! And remember . . . ?"

"God's watching, I know." Estervina kissed her mother on the cheek and swung her apron off. She snatched the drink out of José's hand and walked right past him. Already, she was laughing with a group of girls on the corner.

José chased behind her. He slid a hand around her waist.

"Ey now, mami, you know that drink comes with a price."

"Oh, yeah? What price, José?" She rolled eyes at her girlfriends as she spoke.

"Why don't you come sit with me a while and find out, nena?" His voice, cracking a little, was now projecting into her right ear.

Her friends broke into a fit of giggles. He tightened his grip on her waist.

"Ay, chulo, I think I'd sooner get with your brother. The little one. He's cute!" She swatted his hand away as the girlfriends held their stomachs, cackling. Suddenly, José had a headache. He reached down and snatched her wrist abruptly before his mind turned into a black abyss. She stared at him with a question in her eyes, unafraid and confused. He dropped her wrist.

Gabriel. Coño.

"Have you seen my brother? Where is he?" José continued walking counter-clockwise berating every face he saw. "Where is he?" Blank faces. The combating stereos were overwhelming now. He passed the same faces again and again. The toddlers and the pregnant girls had found their way back to their beds. Finally, a Haitian man selling masks pointed him down Calle De Santos, the main road, where he said a boy was being pulled. José attributed the awkward wording to the man's foreignness and hoped no one had actually taken his idiot brother.

The walk down the main road was like swimming to the bottom of the ocean, traveling further and further from the light. He passed several cows and a goat and bushes with eyes like the mythical negros de la joya that had haunted his childhood memories, ever since they snatched him from the bed he shared with Christian one Easter morning. He prayed now, as he did then, that their grotesque, tarred faces adorned with dried corn leaves would leave him alone. He also prayed that his throbbing headache would go away. But mostly, he prayed that Gabriel wasn't dead, and he prayed his mother wouldn't kill him. He promised now, as he had then, that he would stop sinning and go to church every day and listen to his parents. He wondered if this was his punishment for lying.

He must have walked four miles before he heard the rolling of a river growing closer. That's when he saw the vague spot of a shadow far ahead of him. "Gabriel!

Gabriel! Gabby?" For all he knew, he was yelling at another goat. José picked up his pace, but the shadow stayed the same size. He wondered briefly if the rum was tricking his eyes.

Then the shadow shrank into the river, swallowed swiftly and whole. It was gone.

"Gabriel?" He launched into a sprint. The river, at the bend in the road where kids without plumbing bathed, and where José had experienced his first kiss with a girl from the fishermen's caves, was now a boiling, black mass. Bubbles rose from where it had swallowed the tiny shadow. Gabriel. How many times had their military father pushed his boys off cliffs to teach them to swim? And how many times had José snatched up a small, sinking hand and thrown it to shore?

José's headache flatlined into a searing ringing in his ears.

* * *

The air was ascending from black to navy as Doña Mabel sleepily received the sight of her eldest son cradling her

spasming, wet baby in his arms. She had begun by asking
what the hell José's crazy ass was thinking coming home
at such hours.

"What happened?"

"I don't know."

"Where are his clothes?"

"I don't know!"

"Don't yell at me, José Belén. Why is he wet?"

"He walked into the river como un loco, like he was
possessed or something. I swear! He keeps . . . fighting
me." A sore was building on the side of his abdomen as
Gabriel swung his arms. His mother grabbed a bucket to
prop the door open for her sons, guiding them inside the
house.

La Doña had a knowing look in her eyes. She cleared
the dining room table, hissing under her breath as she
did so.

"El Diablo. El maldito Diablo coño, que vaina." José
had hardly heard her curse this much, though it seemed
like now she was calling upon the Devil himself. She
appeared more annoyed than anything else. "Put him
down here and help me bring this table outside before

your father hears." As if on cue, José Sr. let out a wall-shaking snore.

They carried a squirming Gabriel to the backyard, setting the wooden table beneath the limón tree. Doña Mabel shuffled back inside the house and returned with a yellowed book the size of a Bible. It was lumpy with dried leaves and a rosary sticking out. She opened it beside her ailing son, flipping through a couple of pages frantically, before setting her hand on her desired page. José stood impatiently, his arms hanging limp and useless.

"Vete, get me a pail of river water," she instructed, while laying the back of her hand over Gabriel´s vibrating forehead.

"You want me to go back there?" A sudden ache ran up José's spine. His mother's only response was a pursed lip. She proceeded to pull out a vial of white substance from her book and pour the powder over Gabriel's face. José recognized when he was out of his depth. "Okay, okay, voy."

He picked up the water bucket from the main room and stepped out the front entrance his mother had propped open. The wooden door slammed closed behind him. José jumped with a start. His exhaustion caught up with him for a moment before he curiously tuned his ears through the rhythmic snores of his father and made out his mother's voice, chanting in perfect church-prayer Latin and some other language he couldn't place. From behind the house, he watched as smoke curled up through the tree branches. There was something unnatural in his brother's violent mannerisms. He realized, now, his mother's intentions, and was thankful for an excuse to leave the scene. The new year's sun would be making an appearance any moment.

José — now José by his own declaration and sometimes "Chito" by a stubborn mother — crouched down and began his second sprint of the night. He ran against the clocks ticking within the hearts of the town's roosters. He ran against his father's dreams. He ran and he wondered, hypothetically, how much time he would save not running. How much easier it would be to not be Gabriel Belén's older brother. Then, he ran from the Devil on his heels.

IV.
Cut Day

The speakers in every classroom at John F. Kennedy High School let out a high-pitched beep at 8:23 in the morning. It was a slightly off high E that rang like a dog whistle in every student's ears. Daya Belén was buried in her desk, halfway to sleep, as she often was in her Advanced Spanish class. She was growing tired of this school and Paterson and Jersey in general. Every day there was some new bullshit. New gossip, new police sirens, new rules, and new principals. And today, of all days, an emergency ring from the speakers.

*STUDENTS AND STAFF, PLEASE BE AWARE THAT
WE ARE CONDUCTING A LOCKDOWN. FOLLOW
PROCEDURES UNTIL FURTHER NOTICE.*

The students in Room L10 let out a collective groan.
Second period had hardly even started yet and there were
still a couple kids roaming in the hallways. Daya heard
some guys laughing in the hallway outside their door.

"MOTHERFUCK!" One of them shouted through the
nearly empty hallways.

"Güey, shut the fuck up!" "You're such a dickass!
Shhh!" Every *fuck* was music to Daya's ears. She
commended the creative use of *dickass*.

"Quiet, please!" their blonde substitute teacher
hissed into the hallway before slamming the classroom
door shut. Daya was sure that there was a rule or
something about teachers having to let students in during
a lockdown. She sensed that the woman was new — she
seemed scared of them and was doing a bad job of hiding
it. "Okay! I'm sure you all know what to do. Let's move,
guys!"

Daya waited until more of her classmates got out of

their seats before she grabbed her phone and walked to the back of the room. She crouched under the back table between the only two people she talked to in this class. And the only reason she was taking a class on a language she already knew. A minute of silence passed after the sound of shuffling subsided. Two girls near the window were the first ones to start whispering. And then the whispers spread through the huddle of thirty students like a plague.

"Do you think it's a gun or like a bomb scare again?" Yasmin asked nonchalantly. Daya pretended not to notice the boy behind Yasmin's shoulder passing around a water bottle that was clearly filled with vodka. If there was one thing Daya knew, it was when to mind her business.

"They don't have lockdown drills this early, plus we already had one this month. So, it's probably one or the other. Or just a random guy walking around," Daya answered. She pulled out her phone and refreshed Twitter for updates.

"Freddie said the VP's office said something about someone finding a gun." Amara presented her phone to the group. Daya cursed under her breath. She looked at the clock that was a ticking bomb across the room.

"We can still leave at 8:40 after this is over," Daya asserted. Her friends averted their eyes. "We're still leaving, right?"

"I dunno, dude," Yasmin said, as she pulled a stray hair back into her hijab. "I'm not trynna die over Senior Cut Day."

"Ugh, I don't understand the point of these lockdowns. Anyone can see us through the windows or through the door window . . . like . . . what are we even supposed to do?" Amara gestured towards their nervous substitute, whose leg was rapidly bouncing up and down on her chair. "Ms. Becky finna take a bullet for us?"

A moment later the door handle's violent shaking caused the substitute teacher to jump and directed everyone's attention to the front.

"Yo, it's just the VP check, miss," a boy announced from the back of the group.

"Miss *Haddison*," the woman corrected.

"Whatever, miss."

A couple of students chuckled. Then the whispers

started up again. When Daya refreshed her Twitter, she saw a new article in the North Jersey paper on a student-teacher scandal from the week before. She pinned the article to read later.

"Look, I got twenty bucks and my coupon book. We could hit up Banana King or the Burger Joint or something and then watch a movie. I got a buy-one get-one free for Skylight Cinemas. Let's just go." Daya continued her plea. Even though she already had their whole day planned out, she wanted to make it seem like they had a choice.

"I'm good with whatever," Amara said with a sigh. "Pero ya tú sabe como se pone e'ta." She nodded her head towards Yasmin.

"I don't know how many times I gotta tell you to stop talking shit about me. Arabic and Spanish aren't that different, bitch," Yasmin quipped. She bucked at Amara and the two exchanged a playful look.

"So you're coming?" Daya had been looking forward to this day for weeks. Every year the senior class would attempt to coordinate an official cut day, and every year the organizers would disagree and everyone would just cut class on different days of the same week. Daya preferred it that way, anyways. Wasn't the point of a cut day that no one would know to expect it? And if she left early enough, she could chill with Yasmin and Amara and still make her regular shift at the daycare she worked at in the afternoons. After that, she would work her unpaid shift taking care of her nephew at home.

The sound of heavy footsteps running down the hall brought everyone's attention back to the door.

"If that was the shooter running, don't you think there's gonna be hella police everywhere watching us?" Yasmin was at it again.

"There's already hella police in this school every day, so what? We take the exit near the band room. There's a million kids here. No one's gonna notice." Daya had an answer ready for each and every one of her friend's concerns. "I don't know why you're worried. You're going to Princeton. You're all set."

"Exactly why I can't go to jail!" Yasmin retorted. "Unlike y'all, I actually have something to lose."

"Okay, calm down, that one hurt," Amara said. "You

lucky you're a smart shit and Daya's got her cello. I'd give anything to have a talent."

"Shut up! You have a lotta talents, Amara." Daya punched Amara's shoulder.

"Like what?"

"Uh . . ." Daya and Yasmin looked at each other for help.

"Y'all ain't shit."

"Oh, I know! You can twerk. I wish I could twerk!" said Yasmin, finally, looking proud of herself.

"Yeah, I can't wait to major in twerking at Passaic County Community College." Amara was stone-faced. "Might as well've said rolling blunts. At least I can monetize that."

Daya wasn't sure what to say. She'd never considered that she might be lucky to know what she wanted to do with her life. She didn't really have to think twice about wanting to study music. The hardest part had been telling her parents, but they were mostly just glad that Rutgers awarded her a full scholarship. It was a miracle only God could have given them—finally, one of their children would go to college. Before she got the letter she had no idea how she would get out of Paterson. Daya wanted to tell Amara that everything in her life would work itself out just fine, too, but that didn't feel completely true. She really had no idea what would happen in a month when they all graduated. If she thought about it for too long, it might absolutely terrify her.

So, instead, she pulled up her phone again and found her peers retweeting the news article with variations of #FreeMrWill and #AlanasAThot. She took a deep breath to calm the anger that was bubbling within her. The same thing happened every time a male teacher slept with a student. Despite never personally knowing any of the girls involved, Daya felt the same way each time. She didn't want to deal with it right now.

The ticking hands in the clock aligned with Daya's controlled breathing. She checked her phone one more time before putting it down. 8:37. She really hoped the lockdown wouldn't go into the next period.

"Okay, focus, people. Are we in or are we out?" She kept her eyes on the clock.

"She's in," said Amara. "So is Freddie."

"Fine," Yasmin finally caved.

Daya tugged at the jade beads on the bracelet her late grandmother had given her. She silently prayed that the shooter or the bomb or whatever evil spirits were out there would vanish. As she promised God she would find time to go to Wednesday night mass, Daya filtered through thoughts of the pure, uninhibited freedom she would feel as soon as she stepped foot into the parking lot. The way her heart would race through her chest. The thrill of finally escaping the center of unbridled chaos that was her underfunded, overcrowded high school (a chaos she was sure she would probably miss by next year). The relief of being well into the next week and having today's crisis replaced by another one.

At 8:39, a high E rang through the speakers and released the tension that had been building in the room. At 8:40, the bell rang again to end the period. By 8:45, Daya was standing at a stoplight, calling Skylight Cinemas for showtimes.

V.
Vamo 'pa la Playa

Hidalpa was so small it was left off of many maps of the country. But the town's beaches were on nearly every tourist pamphlet and commercial for the Caribbean nation. Still, the tourists hadn't been able to find it. Probably too far out from the capital city and too close to Haiti for their comfort. It didn't help that there was only one hotel in town, either. And hotel was a strong word. More like a five-bedroom home with amenities like free premium bottled water for bathing, the self-proclaimed best arepa cakes in the country, and a family of street cats living in the kitchen.

The Belén kids weren't staying in a hotel; that would

be an insult to their family name. They were staying at
Don José and Doña Mabel´s house on the corner of Calle
de Santa Mercedes y Calle de Las Águilas. Everyone in
town just called them El Don y La Doña — it seemed like
they were everyone's grandparents, regardless of relation.
Giancarlos, instead of running the streets like other boys,
spent most of his days in the Don's colmado. Every other
morning he earned a couple pesos helping the old man
bring in shipments from the soda trucks. Weekends, he
regularly worked the counter. He had kept his distance
when the old couple's children and grandchildren had
come to visit that summer of '04. But he was always
diligently watching from across the street.

Giancarlos didn't know how to be a kid. He was
always working and hanging out with adults. It didn't
help that he never had any siblings, nor that he had been
abandoned at a young age by an alcoholic birth mother.
He'd been found as an orphan at age six crying in the back
of a broken-down Ford truck by Christian Belén and his
second wife, Luciana Rosario. When Christian proved
unfaithful, Luciana kissed an eight-year-old Giancarlos
on the cheek, before leaving for the city in the middle of

the night with all her belongings. And then it was just him and Christian, less an adoptive parent and more of a roommate and advisor.

When Giancarlos turned ten, Christian asked him, "You ever had a beer, little man?" He then brought Giancarlos along to a bar crawl with the other townies. He never let Giancarlos call him anything other than "Christian" (sometimes he got away with "Señor Christian," but most times that would get him slapped). Whenever Christian had women over, he would put a giant tire in front of the one-room brown shack they called home. And Giancarlos would have to knock on neighbors' doors all night to find a bed. His last resort was El Don y La Doña, but he absolutely hated waking them. He could picture the old woman reluctantly creeping out of her slumber, against gravity and her dwindling health. But she would always let him in, he knew she would.

Since the Belén kids arrived, Christian spent morning and night at the house across the street, his childhood home. His first wife and his four children (two girls, two boys) were there, visiting from Puerto Rico. They didn't talk to Giancarlos past acknowledgment of his

presence in a room. Christian's two brothers were also
there, from New York, along with six children between
them, all girls. Other than baby Ana, they were all more or
less Gian's age. He didn't talk much to them either. They
would just stare at him quizzically as he passed through
Doña Mabel's kitchen at suppertime to pick up a plate.
He never knew what they were thinking. Or what they
were saying, even, with the harsh, squawking English
that sometimes emerged from their mouths. Maybe they
were staring at the stark blackness of his skin, or maybe
they were confused as to his relation to the family. He
was just as confused. His whole life was confusion and
unanswered questions, but he tried not to dwell on it.

Giancarlos watched from behind the curtain as the
Belén kids hung around the front porch at the crack of
dawn, with sleepy eyes and colorful American beach
towels around each of their necks.

"Yo tengo hambre, man!" Daya was the middle
child of José Belén Jr.'s crew of girls. Her hair was done
up in various braids adorned with colorful plastic balls.
Giancarlos noticed she seemed to be the comedian of
the younger bunch. Sometimes he didn't understand the

jokes he overheard but her expressions made him laugh anyways. She even made El Don laugh, which was no small feat. She sat on top of a blue cooler with a pout on her face.

"We're eating when we get there. I packed sandwiches. Donde, carajo, are the Puerto Ricans? They really think they grown, I swear. Where'd they go?" A fatherly Gabriel stood around wearing his fanny pack and waving a plastic bag full of snacks he'd just nabbed from the family store. He stared down the empty street in search of Christian's kids.

"They left, they said they knew the way. Laura went too," explained his daughter, Cristabel, in her cartoonish squeaky voice from a few feet below him. Laura was Gabriel's eldest, only fourteen, but you'd think she was at least eighteen by looking at her.

"Maldito jóvenes de la mierda . . . Why didn't she take y'all with them?"

"I dunno, Pa. We're waiting for Yolanda, she's still in the shower." Cristabel was a very logical little girl. Her mannerisms always made Gian chuckle. She began rubbing sunscreen lotion on her face.

Yolanda, Cristabel, and Daya were inseparable. Yolanda was the object of every little boy's affection in the town, garnering various whistles and catcalls. With Cristabel and Daya by her side, though, the boys were no match. For every whistle there was a comeback from Daya or the rare deep cut from Cristabel. They teased Giancarlos's street-rat friends relentlessly, running through the neighborhood throwing rocks and swatting sticks at them. They lorded their Americanness around like princesses. Benevolent ones, though. Every other night they used the American money they'd exchanged for pesos to buy frío frío for all the neighborhood kids. Back then, a US dollar was worth about forty Dominican pesos, but the price of the sweet ice treat was still one peso. The three girls might as well have been millionaires. Gian never took the frío frío he was offered, he didn't like taking money from girls.

The cry of a baby and an angry wife inside brought Gabriel's frantic energy back towards the house. He paced in circles like a chicken with its head cut off for a moment, unsure of what crisis to handle first. Then he looked directly into the eyes of Giancarlos across the street.

Instantly, the curtain closed and he felt his face redden.
Oh, God. He ran across the room and crouched on top
of the bed, bracing himself for an ass-whupping. Never
in his entire career of people-watching had he ever so
blatantly been caught.

A knock came from the front door. Gian tried not to
breathe.

"I know you're in there, papi, come on out." Gabriel's
voice didn't seem angry.

Gian cracked the door open, leaving the lock chain
between them.

"¿Qué tal, Señor Belén? Buen día," Giancarlos said as
cordially as he could.

"Hola, papi. Listen, I have a proposal for you. Could
you keep an eye on the girls and walk them over to Playa
de Tortuga? Just be their bodyguard, make sure they're
safe. I gotta take care of the baby and set up the food with
Christian. You're coming with us to the beach right?"

Giancarlos's mouth hung open. He couldn't think of a
response.

"Come on, hurry. Go get your bathing suit, I think
they want to leave soon. I can tell que Daya ya se 'tá

poniendo brava. She's got that pout going on." He left Giancarlos at the door and ran back towards the sound of the crying baby.

Giancarlos obliged and quickly grabbed his towel and the key to his bike lock. He didn't bother telling Señor Gabriel that he didn't own a bathing suit.

* * *

Giancarlos made sure to keep a distance of at least ten feet behind the girls as they went down the middle of the empty street. When they stopped running, he started walking slowly beside his bicycle, careful not to intrude or overstep his boundaries. It was the first time he'd been left alone with any girls. He felt a bit nervous around them. Daya walked backwards on her heels and asked him what his name was.

"Giancarlos." He gave her a slight bow. Daya nodded, narrowed her eyes at him, and then spun back around. He felt like he had accidentally revealed something about himself. It was only fair, though — he knew all of their names already. Yolanda muttered something in English and they started laughing. He knew the girls were talking about him. He hung back even further.

Cristabel looked over her tiny shoulder. "Enjoying the view?" she hollered at him. Daya almost doubled over laughing.

They were superior to him in nearly every way — nationality, language, education, class, family, color, beauty. And yet, he was the only one among them who knew the quickest route to Playa de Tortuga, forcing him to speak up in order to give directions. The girls stopped at a split in the road where the gravel began giving way to dirt.

Yolanda whipped her curls around. "Now what do we do?"

"Right," he said, in his best English. He'd picked up a bit from watching Yankee baseball in those bars Christian dragged him to. He regretted the ugly, foreign word the instant it came out, but tried to smile through it.

"¿Tu habla inglés? Wow! You heard that? 'Rrr-ight!'" Daya's rolling r's sparked another wave of giggles from the girls. Giancarlos rolled his eyes, but was not offended. It was his own fault, really.

"Leave him alone, Daya," said Yolanda once her laughing subsided. "Where'd you learn that?"

The light reflected gold in her eyes as she addressed him.

He stuttered, "E-E-En la televisión,"

Yolanda nodded in approval. "See, he's smart! Isn't that right, Giancarlos?"

Gian paused for a beat, raising a brow.

"Of course, mi amor." He bowed his head towards her confidently. She seemed pleased with this. Princesses liked to be treated like princesses, he thought.

They kept walking in better spirits, sharing similar quips and one-word answers. The path took them through a dry forest now, with the rolling waves from the beach growing louder. Playa de Tortuga was named such because from above, it looked like the outline of a tortoise, with a large mound of small sea rocks at its center separating one side of the beach from the other. Beyond the rocks was the finest, softest, whitest sand on the island.

They finally reached la playa — beautiful, peaceful, untouched, and shimmering in the morning light. It

was too peaceful. It was empty. Where were the Belén
teenagers who had gone ahead of them?

The sisters and cousin wandered the empty sand
while Gian watched with his bike from the dry forest.
He looked along the horizon. He noticed some familiar
blobs splashing around on the other side of the turtle
shell — that's what the local kids called the mound of
rocks that split the beach. It seemed almost endless if you
were standing in front of it, and going around it meant
brushing against thorned shrubs or trudging back to take
another route to that side of the beach. The quickest way
to the other side was through the rocks.

Giancarlos hesitated. There was an ache in his
stomach that prevented him from stepping further. He
wasn't sure if Señor Gabriel would approve of going to the
far side of the beach. It was a longer walk and a deeper
ocean, and sometimes kids from his school would tell
stories about the sharks that lived on the far side of the
beach. Or about the older kids who would go there in the
middle of the night and do older-kid activities. He let out
a sigh, seeing no other option.

"¡'Tan por ahi!" He pointed to the horizon beyond the

rocks. "Come on, I'll help you chicas go through the rocks. Watch your step."

"Are you sure?" said Yolanda.

"Ay, can't we go around?" asked Daya, already out of breath. Giancarlos shook his head in the negative.

He held each girl's hand one by one as they walked barefoot through the mess of rocks, looking for the roundest ones to place their feet on and averting a couple broken bottles.

"Coño!" Cristabel let out a curse as she stepped down off the last couple of round rocks before they reached the sand. Giancarlos's eyes widened. She assured him she was fine, perfectly fine, forget about it. It was just a prick. He ripped off a piece of his oversized T-shirt anyways and wrapped it expertly around Cristabel's heel. Just in case.

They continued walking towards the elder cousins, their splashing and shrieks growing louder with every step. Giancarlos's tension eased the closer they got. He'd never experienced belonging to a tribe like this. They all fit together like a scene out of a novela. It was intoxicating. The smell of salt mixed with affectionate splashes shimmering in the sun. The beach was so close to his shack, yet he'd never even dipped his toe in the water before. People did this for fun? Giancarlos reached hip-level ocean and sank his head lower, taking in a large gulp of salt water. He tilted his head back, attempting to float.

Not even fifteen minutes passed before another howling "Coñooo!" was heard. This time it was from Daya. The sound of wailing tears put an abrupt stop to any friendly splashing, and by the time Giancarlos stood up to regain his senses, one of the older cousins had already carried her out of the water. Giancarlos swam as fast as he could back to shore. Yolanda and Cristabel rushed to huddle around her. Cristabel caught sight of the ten four-inch red spikes poking out of her cousin's foot and went to go lie down on a towel. Daya must have stepped on a guanábana. Giancarlos did not envy her. He cursed himself for not listening to the bad feeling in his stomach sooner. And if it wasn't bad enough, Crista began crying now too. Jesus Christ. She had unwrapped the fabric Giancarlos put around her heel to reveal a foot more swollen than a spring pig. The pain must've subsided in the saltwater and now it was catching up to her. *El Diablo*, thought Gian. *Two of them.*

Almost on cue, a black motorcycle sped through the sand, making its way towards them. It was Christian, riding recklessly in like a knight in shining armor, without a helmet or clean shirt. Giancarlos simultaneously felt both relief that an adult was there and fear at the questions that would be asked. But Christian simply scooped the two injured girls onto the back of his bike, and told them to hold on. Daya squeezed her uncle hard and dampened the back of his wrinkled tank top with her tears. Giancarlos followed behind them as fast as he could pedal.

Once the girls were delivered to the local hospital — four rooms and a front desk — Giancarlos buried his face in Christian's sweaty arms. He couldn't help it. It was all his fault.

"No, no, no. Why are you crying? Boys don't cry, you heard?" Christian steadied the shirtless child before him, holding him by the slumped shoulders. "Why are you crying?"

Giancarlos tried to find his voice. The tears kept streaming.

"P-Porque . . . you're gonna get rid of me, right? I

didn't do my job good and now you're sending me back to
la calle . . . Back to the street where I belong, right? Please,
please, Christian, let me stay. I'll work the store every day,
I'll clean your motorcycle, please!"

Christian met Giancarlos' eyes with a piercing
directness. He shook the boy's shoulders violently.

"Muchacho! Tu 'ta loco, eh? What the hell are you
talking about. Ya, stop with that. Stop it." Christian took
off his white tank top and handed it to the boy. "Here,
fix yourself. Now, listen. I can't get rid of you, all right?
¿Entiendes? Not even if I wanted to. You may not be mine,
but you're a Belén, all right, negrito? I won't say this lightly
and I'm not gonna say it again. You got me?"

Giancarlos finished wiping his tears. He stopped
sobbing and started nodding fervidly. As detached as
it sounded coming out of his mouth, this was the most
earnest Christian had ever been towards him or any of his
own children. Christian let go of the boy and squared his
broad shoulders.

"Alright, damn."

VI.
Payphone

The first time Franklyn's mother found "la marijuana" in his room, she convinced his father to send him away for a month to his aunt's house back in the Dominican Republic. The threat of being sent back had always loomed over the six boys in a joking tone throughout their three years living in New York. His brothers regularly waltzed into the tiny top floor of their three-family home drunker than hell, but this latest infraction turned out to be the final straw that caused Mami to keep true to her word.

Franklyn's parents had funny rules. They didn't make sense to him most of the time. Drinking was fine. Encouraged, even. Missing curfew meant a good amount of yelling (but his family communicated at a high volume anyways). A teen pregnancy was discouraged but fixable — easily spun into a gift from God. Hip-hop and "esa musica de esos negritos" was the work of the Devil. Marijuana was a sin.

And so Franklyn was sent away at age fourteen to reflect on his crime. Even at that age, and even knowing that he would return at the end of that August, the young man still shed multiple tears all the way along his walk to the bus stop. He had to sit through two bus rides to Miami, wedged between two pieces of luggage for a day, and then catch a red-eye with the ticket his father had gotten from some cousin or uncle who worked at Miami International. His cheeks remained wet as he woke up to the intense sunlight hitting Las Américas International Airport. Then another bus ride on the island stuffed between a baby-wielding woman and an upset, caged hen spinning feathers into the air.

He absorbed all the dormant night clubs and markets and flying motorcycles that suddenly surrounded him. It was like another dimension. Something like the Heights, but also something entirely new. A glimpse into the life he could be leading if his parents had made different decisions. He had never spent more than an hour in Santo Domingo. It wasn't the dirt and field countryside he was used to seeing near his childhood hometown on the other side of the island. Perhaps, he thought, he could spin this punishment in his favor. A month in Santo Domingo. If he were white, this would be a vacation.

- Maritza -

Her baby cousin had lost none of his doe-eyed newborn qualities since the last time Maritza had seen him six years ago. He stuck out like the tourist that he was at the bus station. He was in a daze, desperate to the point of being about to ask an obvious pickpocket for help, before Maritza's mother scooped him into an embrace.

"¡Mi niño! ¡Mi bebecito!" Her mami covered his tiny pale face in red lipstick and stroked every inch of it with her plastic red nails.

Maritza couldn't help but laugh at his stupid, bewildered look.

"Hola, Tía Lupe. Bendición, Tía,"

Lupe returned his bendiciones.

Maritza took the opportunity to grab his lip-stained cheeks and pinch them as hard as she could.

"¡Primitoooo! Ay que lindo!"

He squirmed away, but she caught him in a chokehold beneath her armpit before he could escape. Those years Maritza had spent lifting weights for volleyball seemed almost worth it. She remembered playing with an infant Franklyn when she was young. He was her little toy. Now here he was, almost a man.

"What, you don't love your cousin anymore, Lyndito?"

Franklyn stopped resisting.

"Leave my baby alone, Maritza. ¿Y eso? Act like a lady!" Her mother's voice shifted into its usual stern tone. She was an entirely different person when they had guests.

Maritza tried to resist rolling her eyes, but her body put up a good fight. Surely, when her brother Tito had put her into a chokehold when they were kids, their mother had simply scoffed it off. Pero her? A girl? Shit, she could never do anything. At least with Lyndo here, she figured she wouldn't be the baby of the family anymore.

As they walked from the bus stop to their home, Maritza noticed her baby cousin lose some of the spark he'd had upon arrival. It was a fifth-floor walk-up above a bar. Her mother had to swipe away trash and empty bottles of Presidente in order to open the front door. Maritza was sure his life in the States, with all the celebrities and baseball players in Nueva York, was much more glamorous than this.

His spark dimmed all the way down in the weeks that followed, as her mother began treating him like a regular family member, assigning him all the laundry washing and the trips to the water shop four miles uphill every morning to pick up the daily supply. And in the afternoon, when her father and brother got home from the factory, they tossed their work boots at him for polishing. Her parents had put him to work so quick, Maritza knew he had to have done something bad to be sent all by himself. Drugs, probably.

Pobrecito.

- Franklyn -

After one week of being an on-call servant in his aunt's house, Franklyn was exhausted. But he didn't complain. At least he had a roof over his head, fresh mangoes every day, and an ice-cold Presidente every night. And Tía's food, which wasn't as good as his mother's, but definitely showed similar influences. And he got to watch as his cousins — older, wiser, and nicer to him than his own brothers — showed off their skills as rebellious young adults. He marveled at them.

In the States, his house felt like it was better secured than any federal prison. But Tía Lupe wasn't the German shepherd watchdog his mother was. And boy did his cousins take advantage.

Normally, only one could sneak out at a time, as it would require either Maritza or Tito to stay behind and drop the rickety fire-escape ladder down outside Tito's room as quietly as possible so the other could return from their escapades. If they woke their parents, they would be more outraged at the fact that they had been disrupted from their sleep than at the trickery of their children. In such a case, there would be hell to pay. But the system was so perfected that this rarely ever happened.

And now that Franklyn was in the picture, both Maritza and Tito could go live their double lives frequently and simultaneously. Franklyn was never invited — he looked too young for the bouncers to even pretend to believe he was eighteen.

In a blinding black space one night, the two cousins expertly made their escape. After tiptoeing past their parents' bedroom and avoiding the creaking floorboards they knew by memory, maneuvering down the fire escape was the next challenge. Maritza, carrying a shimmering silver dress and silver handbag in one hand, white knockoff brand platforms in the other. Tito, carrying his broad shoulders along with the money he'd been hiding from his father and a confident strip of condoms in his back pocket.

Franklyn looked wistfully out the window for a moment. He wondered if he'd ever really know what it was like out there. Then, he reached into his backpack and pulled out the marked-up copy of Dante's *Divine Comedy* he'd gotten from his ESL teacher in New York.

– Maritza –

At the bottom, Tito ran off in the direction of one of his girlfriends' houses and Maritza was received by a woman dressed in all black, leaning against the brick wall of the alleyway. Her makeup was drawn by a more experienced hand, evident even in the dim light cast by the cigarette between her fingers. She had a knowing grin on her face.

"Por fin, I thought you chickened out."

Blanca was Maritza's favorite older cousin from her father's side. Maritza thought she was a bit reckless. Jackie, a short-haired girl from the building across the street, almost ran into a motorcyclist on her way to meet them. Light from the flickering streetlamp above them bounced off her gold latex dress. The trio made their way to Blanca's boyfriend's car, waiting at the corner. He was a bit reckless too, thought Maritza. The whole situation made her nerves tense, but she was determined to ignore them tonight. Word was that a bunch of Navy men had just arrived from their time at sea and were hanging out at the local Discoteca X two blocks away. Perfect time for Maritza to finally get a boyfriend.

Several lies to a Cuban bouncer and five drinks later.

Blanca was nowhere to be seen. Neither was her boyfriend. The air was thick with the smell of sweat and liquor. A blue strobe light pulsed around the packed dance floor. Strangers spun around each other like they'd been friends and lovers for decades. Maritza found Jackie sitting at a booth, crowded by several men in uniform. A pang of jealousy hit her. Why did men never come up to her? Was she intimidating or something? Or was it because she wasn't stick thin like Jackie and actually had some muscle on her? Her father always said men liked their girls strong. She wedged herself between Jackie and a tall soldier with a pink scar across his cheek.

Three drinks later and Maritza felt the floor come out from beneath her. The pink scar spoke elegant

Spanish and offered her a bubbly drink through clouds of smoke. Maritza didn't have time to refuse. Her stomach immediately took her legs to the nearest musty bathroom.

One empty stomach later.

Jackie was no longer Jackie. Maritza's head was too muddled to figure out why. She laughed at the goofy grin on her friend's face. Where was Blanca?

- Franklyn -

A light tapping of a rock on the door prompted Franklyn to turn on the dim light in his older cousin's bedroom and open the window. It was around three in the morning. A relatively short night. Maybe an unsuccessful one? He carefully unlatched and rolled down the stairs. In a moment, Tito was standing before him with a satisfied grin, kicking Franklyn off his place on the bed and onto his blanket on the floor. Franklyn obliged, as usual. Definitely a good night, then.

- Maritza -

Maritza decided she didn't like alcohol anymore. Not tonight. No more trips to the pee-stained bathroom. She got up to get a glass of water from the bar. Her nerves advised her not to trust the pink scar to get it for her.

She turned back with a cup of water in hand to find that the damn short-haired tipa had disappeared. She spotted Jackie being led towards the door by the tall soldier and his friend. Where the hell was Blanca? Maritza followed outside and found her small friend in the backseat of a brown Cadillac.

"We're just giving her a ride home," Just being gentlemen, naturally. Maritza decided she wanted a ride home, too. They were sisters, she said. She joined her new sister in the backseat of the brown Cadillac.

After forty-five minutes, Maritza felt a jolt. It was as if she'd been drowning and finally could gasp for air. They were not going home. Home was thirty minutes ago. She was alone in this car. Jackie was drugged. Blanca was gone. Her purse carried only her blue eye shadow, crimson lipstick, a used tissue, and a tin box of Altoids. She did not know these two men in the front seat. She had to go to church in the morning. She would probably die tonight. Maritza slowly grabbed her sister's black clutch. Inside she found a pack of cigarettes, a condom, a compact mirror, and their only hope. A single peso coin. A stray payphone zoomed past them. They were in the middle of nowhere.

Maritza forgot she also carried something else. The stern voice of her mother. The infamous pestering spirit that had always annoyed her, yet ran heavily through the blood in her veins.

"I have to pee."

"Almost there, mi amor."

"I HAVE TO PEE. Let me out of this car or I will piss on your goddamn velvet seats."

"Crazy bitch."

On the side of the road, in still darkness, she was now truly alone and at least half a mile from the payphone with the dead weight of Jackie's cumbersome body to carry. Years from now she would look back on this night of her shared eighteenth birthday and wonder how the hell she fought through the aching in her bones and survived.

Upon reaching the promised land, she realized she only knew one number from memory. A curse escaped her breath.

". . . Mamá?"

"Habla Franklyn. Maritza? Where are you?"

"Oh thank god."

"Shit, I think I hear Tía y Tío getting up. I can tell them it was a wrong number, though. Are you okay, prima?"

Maritza felt her voice shaking. She took an unsteady breath.

"No . . . it's okay . . . Put her on."

VII.
Bárbaro

*E*arly in the morning on the twenty-third of February, every resident of la Avenida Eduardo Conde was awoken by the blaring of a red Ford F-150 adorned with a Puerto Rican flag on the rear window. Occasionally, the man driving the truck would honk at nothing. It wasn't an unusual occurrence. In fact, it was the opposite of unusual. It was familiar and dependable. As dependable as seeing drunk American tourists overflowing out of each corner of San Juan every spring break.

ESTE DOMINGO, PUERTO RICO CELEBRA LA UNIDAD CARIBEÑA CON LA TERCERA PARADA

DOMINICANA. TE ESPERAMOS EN LA AVENIDA
PONCE DE LEÓN EN SAN JUAN.

The radio announcer's voice repeated the message over and over again from the speakers of the truck. It was the siren that called every tía on their street to Rita Salón that morning to have themselves transformed into something entirely new for the Dominican Day Parade. Rita, herself, was halfway through her own transformation, with five mini rollers hanging loosely in her hair and only one hand of painted red nails done.

"Yoanson Joel DeLeón-Belén! You hear me calling you!" Rita's voice rang throughout the salón. Despite historically being beaten or berated when he heard his middle name spoken, Yoanson closed the Game Boy Advance console that was illuminating his face in the dark staff bathroom. He slipped the device into his pocket and pushed open the crooked pink door in front of him.

"Yoanson!"

His mother grew impatient. He walked up behind her, dodging clouds of heat and the putrid smell of burnt hair. There was barely room for him to move. Yoanson

studied his mother, whose hands were wound up in
Señora Judy's red bob. The mini rollers in her own hair
were hanging on for dear life. She was a woman who was
always waiting to let her hair out — waiting for an event
or an appointment or someone worthwhile. Yoanson
didn't understand why she spent hours every week sitting
in an inferno just to cover her hair up the next day. Like
she was saving up every last ounce of her beauty for the
day she would finally need it.

"Yoanson!"

He rolled his eyes, watching her look everywhere BUT
his direction.

"I'm right here."

Rita jumped as if he were a tiny ghost.

"Papito, how many times have I told you to take
a bath and get ready? Look at you . . ." She grabbed
Yoanson's shoulders roughly, and turned them around.
"You look like a brujito. What is this?" She pulled at the
hair standing stiffly above his head. His teenage sister,
Emely, stifled a laugh from under a hooded dryer. He
stuck his tongue in her direction.

"I don't have time for this. Go put your sneakers on.

José's outside waiting for you." She shooed him away with her free hand. Yoanson slowly turned his head towards the glass doors at the front of the salón. A lanky stranger stood behind the glass, smoking a cigarette beside a rusted bicycle. She said it like it was nothing. *José's outside.*

"¿Qué lo que, 'manito? You're getting tall, huh?" José gently knocked his fist against Yoanson's jaw. He knew the words were false — he had not grown even a centimeter in at least two years (no matter how hard he tried). Yoanson regarded his brother suspiciously. In his ten years of existence, he could count on his hands the number of times he could remember seeing José in person. Once, he'd asked his eldest sister, Hennessy, why their brother didn't live with them. She'd told him that José had a family of his own in Bayamón and he'd moved there when Yoanson was a toddler. And that was that. His fear of asking a stupid question kept him from asking any more. When he was six, Yoanson remembered someone shoving him a photo of a little girl holding a baby and telling him that those were his sobrinos. But Yoanson didn't yet have the vocabulary to hold the weight of the word *tío.*

"What are you doing here?"

José pointed at the red, white, and blue flag hanging outside their mother's salón.

"I'm Dominican and proud, remember?"

"You weren't so proud last year." Yoanson crossed his arms. José chuckled.

"I guess I was busy."

Yoanson wondered at his brother's secret life. At all the ways he found to stretch the boundless limits of his freedom. He had the whole island to explore and come home to at any time he pleased. All the while, leaving Yoanson behind — alone and defenseless against a tribe of women.

"Aight, Yo-Yo, Imma be honest here. Ma wants me to take you to the barber," José said. Yoanson couldn't picture his mother asking José for anything. He'd barely ever seen her talk to him on the phone. Maybe one of his sisters had asked him. They kept trying to cut his hair or straighten it, but he wouldn't let anyone touch it. Yoanson thought about turning back into the crowded salón and continuing his game of *Sonic*.

"There's this place down the street I used to go to."

José swung his leg over his bicycle and patted his hand on the seat. "Vámono'."

Yoanson sighed deeper than a ten-year-old should have to before hopping on and gripping his fingers on the bike frame. By the time they arrived at their destination, he was sure his hair had doubled in size. He felt it moving freely through the air around him.

The hand-painted sign above them read "Tony's Barber Shop," and a headshot of David Ortiz with a fresh cut was plastered to the window. It was a familiar storefront Yoan passed every time he walked to the supermarket two blocks further.

"You've never been here before?" José asked, as he carried his brother off the bike. Yoanson would have rather dismounted by himself.

"No," he replied gruffly. "Mami cuts my hair at the salon."

Yoanson was immediately stunned at how much of a baby this made him sound like. He wished he had been able to come up with some lie instead. It had been years since his mother had even cut his hair. Never once, before now, did he even have any desire to get a haircut anywhere

else. He barely ever wanted to get his hair cut at all. He'd
spent all this time growing it — why would he just get
rid of it?

"Hmm . . ." José reached his hand towards Yoan's
head, but was swiftly blocked by a small arm. He paused
for a second before reaching around Yoanson's back and
pushing him along through the chiming door.

"'¿Que lo que', mi gente?" José's booming voice
bounced off the farthest barber's chair and ricocheted
between the walls — where one side was plastered with
Boston Red Sox memorabilia and various Dominican
flags, and the other had images of brown-skinned saints
and multicolored rosaries. Three of the four barbers
working nodded towards José politely, but regarded him
with curious eyes. The other one, dressed in an all-black
fit with the name *Tony* embroidered on his oversized shirt,
dropped his clippers and approached them. The man's
hair was in two braids on the top and shaved on the sides.
A gold chain shifted around his neck. His eyes lit as they
scanned José up and down.

"The prodigal son returns! Diablo, man, I ain't seen
you in years!"

The two men embraced each other. They asked about each other's families and children and jobs and wives, as strangers who were once friends are bound to do. Yoanson zoned out of their conversation as he examined his surroundings. There was a line of five men waiting in plastic chairs, watching the news on the television above them. They ranged from a teenager to an elderly man with red dye dripping off what was left of his hair. Besides the absence of a particular burning-hair smell, Yoan could see how eerily similar this place was to his mother's salón. It was like walking into an alternate universe. In his peripheral, Yoan could see and hear his brother laughing with Tony. Within a minute, Tony took the long black cape off his current client and slipped it onto his brother.

"Yo-Yo, sit tight. Tony's gonna set you up next. He's the only man in San Juan I let anywhere near my scalp." José gave Tony a fist bump as he said this. "Hámelo, uno, tre' y media. And line up my beard just a little."

Yoanson wasn't sure where his body was meant to be. All of the chairs near the door were taken. None of the men even looked him in the eyes or offered up their seat. If he knew where the bathroom was, he would've loved hiding in there. He was about to just sit down on the floor when Tony approached him.

"You Belén's brother? Come, there's a free spot over here." The man pointed to the leather chair at the empty station beside his brother. As soon as he hoisted himself up on the chair, Yoan pulled the GameBoy out of his pocket and immediately resumed collecting Sonic rings while the men talked in circles around him.

* * *

"Romy, relax with that cell phone, man. I'm telling you, the government is listening on that shit," Tony said to the barber texting behind him.

"Tú 'ta loco, man. Te pasa'te con esa vaina," Romy complained, head still in his phone.

"Next he's gon start talkin' 'bout gremlins stealing his shit again. He needs to stop smokin'," another barber chimed in. Tony shook his head.

"See, this why I don't talk to y'all. Y'all don't ever wanna talk about liberation. I'm trynna tell my friend here about systemic oppression under a capitalist anti-Black society, and he hears 'gremlins.' Acting like y'all don't know aliens are real. You know I'm right, that's why you're mad. Don't even front about it. Calling ME crazy . . . right." He kissed his lips and regarded José. "I was talking about los biembienes. You heard of that shit? The little monkey monsters in el campo that come and steal children."

"Yeah, I heard of it. Kid stuff." José tilted his head down as Tony worked on his fade.

"Right, now listen here and then tell me I'm crazy. You know where they came from, right? Where everything comes from: slaves. And — now, look at this — they're dique slaves and Indians who ran away and hid in the mountains and turned into goddamn beasts. Turned into literal animals. To come and eat your kids. Tell me that's not racist."

"I dunno man, you sound kinda crazy." José was laughing now, along with the rest of the shop. Some men were nodding their heads, while others rolled their eyes.

"You're saying my grandmother, black as night, was racist because she told fairy tales?" Romy called out.

"You're not listening." Tony brought a finger to his temple, keeping his focus on José's scalp.

"Tell me again, then, how my country is bad and racist and hates women and never did anything good. Turn around and see you waving the biggest flag at the parade, won't I?"

"You're not listening," he repeated.

"¡Dímelo, entonce! You just wanna keep slandering Dominicans."

"Chacho, you know I don't kiss the United States' colonizer ass either, don't even start. But, you wanna talk about fairy tales. They're not all fairy tales, some of this shit is real. And you gotta know that fairy tales, stories, things we teach kids — these things show our values as a society." Tony regarded the whole shop now, as though he were giving a campaign speech.

"Okay, professor, what does Cinderella show us about society?"

"Pshhh, you threw an easy one. Sexism and classism. Mmmm . . . Dominican as hell. Gimme another."

The whole shop burst into laughter and the men in

the waiting chairs talked over one another. A man shouted from his chair.

"Las sirenas!"

"Sexism again. Women are evil and luring fishermen to their deaths with their looks? You're kidding, right?"

Another man shouted above the ruckus.

"El comegente."

"The serial killer legend. I bet you five hundred dollars he was a Black man, wasn't he? I think he was. Racism, again."

"Mi abuelo dijo que fue negro, sí. Y Haitiano."

The elderly man had spoken up from the waiting line, sitting behind his newspaper. Tony pointed his clippers at the old man in gratitude.

"What did I tell you? Of course he was Haitian. A damn shame."

"What's a damn shame is the Haitians taking over la isla and stealing our jobs," Romy mumbled to his client. Tony spun around and shot Romy a look of disapproval.

"Dímelo, Romy, what do you think e'to Pueltorriqueños think of you walking around with money in your pockets on *their* island? I told you to stop talking that nationalist shit," Tony said.

Yoanson was nearly finished with another level of Sonic before his console powered down. He slammed the black screen shut and cursed at the ceiling, barely able to hear his own thoughts over the uproar. The men in the waiting chairs were all talking over one another, arguing over half-baked politics he had no interest in. They may as well have been speaking another language.

"I'm tired of your communist ass, Tony. I don't know how you can even talk with that long-ass shirt. Man's got on a dress," Romy said, high-fiving the agreeable barber next to him. Yoan noted that the man sitting in Romy's chair was nearly unrecognizable from the man he'd seen when they arrived. His beard was trimmed with razor-sharp precision, like an artist had drawn it on.

"And I don't know how you can talk with them hips," Tony whipped back. The other barbers nearly collapsed at that. One barber just let out a dramatic "HA!" in Romy's sheepish face. Yoan felt like he was watching a circus act. He couldn't help but crack a smile, too. Tony dramatically spun the cape off of José, revealing his finished work.

"Your turn, little man."

José got up from his chair and ran his hands over his freshly cut scalp. He ran his palms across his jaw too as he stared at himself in the mirrored wall. He let out a whistle, pleased. As soon as Yoanson sat in his brother's place, he felt a rush of nerves take a hold of him. There was a spotlight on Tony's chair. It was the center from which the whole shop revolved, and where he felt the heat of a dozen eyes. He remembered feeling similarly last winter when he had to give a speech to his English class.

"What do we want, then?" Tony spoke to Yoan through the mirror in front of them. Yoanson stayed silent, trying to come up with a suitable answer. "Something like your brother, maybe? Or one of these? Just say the word." He pointed to a series of photos with more variations of close-cropped, sharply lined hairstyles. Yoan couldn't imagine himself with any of them.

"Just do him up like me," José chimed in, not breaking eye contact with himself. "¡Ya tu sabe'! You'll be gettin' all the ladies, like your brother, Yo-Yo!"

Tony leaned down and spoke softly over Yoanson's

shoulder. "Is that what you want?" Yoanson shook his head — *no*. Tony ran his hands through Yoanson's hair, inspecting it.

"Bueno, no matter what, we gotta wash this first. Follow me."

When they returned to the chair, Tony combed through his wet hair a couple more times, working in silence as news audio filled the shop. He pumped a mysterious liquid into his hands and ran it through Yoan's tight coils. He ran a smaller comb through his hair again, this time stopping a half inch from the ends.

"You see your ends, right here? They're split and damaged so I'm just gonna trim this much off, okay?"

Yoan nodded tepidly in agreement. He immediately felt the weight on his head shrinking bit by bit. Just as Tony was finishing, José averted his gaze from the TV. The protests began when Tony put the scissors down. Whoa, whoa, whoa. It wasn't short enough, Yoan's estranged brother said, tugging at a coil. He wanted it all off.

"He doesn't want to cut it — I asked," Tony shrugged in reply.

"He doesn't want to eat vegetables either, but sometimes you just have to, no?" his brother replied with laughter in his voice. But Tony was a brick wall — a wall Yoanson looked to in awe.

"Look, he doesn't want to cut it, I'm not gonna cut it. We'll figure something out. Meantime, you can take this"—he slid a folded bill out of his pocket and placed it in José's hand—"and go get two beers from next door. Okay? Cálmate con takeiteasy. Ya 'ta to'." He patted José on the shoulder.

José stood in a moment of shock. His eyes passed between Yoanson and the barber towering half an inch above him. José lowered his voice and looked intently at his old friend.

"Mami's gonna kill me if I bring him back with that on his head," he pleaded.

"Sounds like her problem. Don't even worry about paying, it's on the house. Relájate, bro," Tony said with a smile, guiding José out the door. Finally, José complied, leaving the shop behind him. Yoan was stunned. It was some sort of small magic.

Tony clapped his hands together and brought his attention back to his client.

"It's you and me, Señor Belén."

Yoanson's eyes lit up. His nerves had dissipated into the air, leaving his attention focused on the image in front of him, willing it to grow into something that felt . . . right. Searching for hints at what he was meant to become.

Tony continued.

"How do we feel about braids?"

VIII.
Skipping Stones

One day, we should go on a trip together. Why don't you ever come visit me in New York?" Ana dug her fingers into the fine sand. Zahaira laughed beside her.

"Imagine! Your accent might fool people, but you really are American, nena." Zahaira crouched her legs up and lay on her back with her hands behind her head. The Ray-Bans Ana had let her borrow really did suit her. Ana had already resolved to let her keep them.

"Traveling makes me American?" Ana asked.

"That and the blue hair and white suit," Zahaira smirked. They'd spent all morning setting up the funeral and she hadn't mentioned Ana's new look until now. Ana turned and raised her brows, wondering if she should have come to watch the sunset alone.

"Relájate, loca. I'm kidding, you look good! Like a prince." Zahaira looked up at her, letting her glasses fall to the tip of her nose.

Ana averted her eyes from the young woman's soft gaze and turned back to the gently turning ocean. She swatted away the gnats that were making a feast of her ankles and took a swig of the Presidente bottle beside her. It was the first taste of alcohol she'd had since she landed. It tasted like home. She offered the bottle to Zahaira, even though she knew her friend didn't drink.

"I think we should go to Greece or Thailand. I know a girl from school who went to Thailand and came back a whole new bitch. She cut all her hair off and started meditating and going to yoga every day and collecting crystals and shit. I think I want that. A whole new body."

"That's why you cut your hair?" Zahaira couldn't help herself. Did Ana think she could waltz into a small town like Hidalpa looking like that and no one was gonna make jokes?

"Now I'm starting to get the feeling you got a problem

or something," Ana hugged her knees to her chest, annoyed.

Zahaira sighed. She sat upright and slowly crept her hand up the nape of Ana's neck. The sides were buzzed and on top lay a mop of Ana's signature coils. Zahaira currently had her hair wrapped in a silk scarf, but after a trip to the salon, it trailed past her belly button. She'd been growing it all her life — well, her mother had. As she looped a blue curl around her index finger, Zahaira wondered what it would be like to not feel the extra weight on her head. She retracted her hand quickly, suddenly feeling wrong. Ana's scalp tingled.

It had been almost three years since Ana's last visit. Things between them felt different. Stuck. They were nearly strangers, each wondering how much of the past the other remembered. Zahaira figured the sullen emotions from Ana's grandfather passing surely hadn't helped, but neither had her showing up like . . . this. She noticed the distance between Ana and the Belén family, as well. Ana and her sister, Cristabel, had sat two rows behind the rest of them at the church service.

"I can't go to Greece, or Thailand, or New York,

or Guadalajara. I've barely ever even been outside of Hidalpa," Zahaira spoke in her softest volume, which was most people's regular volume.

"Don't you want to leave?"

"Of course, every day." Zahaira shook her head. Then she laughed again. "You know how long my brother's been waiting on a visa to visit our uncle in Miami? Five years. And still nothing. Not all of us have the luxury of a blue passport."

"Fuck. I'm sorry. I didn't—" Ana turned to look at her sheepishly.

"Para, para, para. Está bien. It doesn't matter. Besides, I have to take care of Mami y quien tiene dinero pa' eso? If I gotta be stuck anywhere, might as well be the most beautiful barrio in the most beautiful country in the world." Zahaira said this with the same smile she wore when they would beg the pica-pollo lady for scraps of leftover chicken as kids. The same dimpled cheeks Ana would incessantly poke her fingers into. She constantly marveled at her friend's ability to smile through nearly any bad situation.

The horizon was turning pink now.

"Anyways, fea, if we were in New York, would they have these?" Zahaira reached into the pocket of her shorts and pulled out a small branch with three balls of green fruit.

Ana's eyes immediately lit up.

"Limoncillos! Ugh, I haven't had these in forever! I used to sit by Abuela's tree and eat bowls and bowls of these. They're my favorite!" Ana gasped and picked a limoncillo off the branch.

"I know," Zahaira said.

* * *

Even though Ana was the youngest of all the American Belén girls, she was the only one of her sisters who spoke Spanish with her parents — at least, that's when they were speaking. Of course, she made mistakes all the time, mixing up *cien* and *mil* and *millones* with each other and referring to a microwave by the wrong gender. But gender was a construct anyways, so she didn't care. She barreled on through her sentences. She laughed at her own stubborn tongue. Ana figured she'd never known how to keep her mouth shut before — why would she let a language stop her now?

She was also the only one who kept taking her parents up on their offers to pay for her plane tickets to Dominican Republic. Every six months or so her father would ask the girls if they wanted to visit their grandparents in Hidalpa. Ana never turned him down. At one point, her older sisters sat her down at a dinner to ask her to stop wasting their money when her parents were struggling to pay their mortgage. She didn't listen. When she begged for an American Girl doll as a child, her parents would pull her away from the window displays and pick up a doll from the 99 Cent Store on their way home. But money was no object for a trip to the island. She knew that no matter how poor they were, unemployed or not, Papi would find the money for plane tickets and would do so gladly. The tickets could have been a million dollars and he would probably take out a loan to pay it with a smile. And Ana couldn't help herself.

On a trip with her father, Ana was on a mission to find grapes at the street market in Hidalpa when a softball the size of her head knocked her square in the back. She must have been five or six, still clinging to the orbit of her grandmother, who was busy talking to a papaya vendor ten feet away.

She remembered she was wearing the yellow dress her abuela had stuffed her into and that she hated it more than anything. The seams pulled at her chubby arms and the tulle was like barbed wire on her thighs. It was just in the way of everything. How was she supposed to run with this thing flapping everywhere and the bow trailing behind her? Then Ana was struck and she met Zahaira, this deep-umber, bony little thing in overalls.

"'Ta lindo, tu vestido," the girl said as she pulled at the ribbon on Ana's waist. And suddenly, Ana had a friend to help her cover the yellow dress in dirt that day.

* * *

"Do you think they loved each other?" Ana asked before spitting out the pit from her last limoncillo. There was juice dripping down her chin.

"Who?" Zahaira rolled her eyes. She hated when they started speaking sincerely.

"My grandparents. It's kind of weird that you probably spent more time with them than I did." Ana had to remind herself not to feel guilty about things she couldn't control.

"I don't know. I don't think they thought about love like that. I think he needed her to take care of him. And in a way, she needed him, too." Zahaira tossed the branch she held across the sand. "And I don't think it matters how much time you spent together. They loved you and your sisters, for sure." Ana loved when her friend dropped her wall of clownery. But she wasn't sure she agreed with the sentiment.

"I don't think they would still love me. Not the same way." Ana directed her attention towards the ocean. They were the words she'd thought about many times while drunk, but never said aloud.

"Don't say that." Zahaira examined the girl. Something about Ana really terrified her — and it wasn't just the hair or the new tattoos poking out from her neck and wrists. " . . . Is it true you're living on your own, without your parents?"

Ana kept her eyes straight ahead.

"I don't know. Is that what the church ladies are saying?"

Ana got up from the sand with the remains of her beer and wandered to the shore, in search of the perfect stone. She found a smooth, grey one and skipped it over the water. Zahaira followed suit beside Ana and threw her own.

* * *

The first time Ana found herself alone at the arrivals gate of Las Américas International Airport, she was sixteen and still searched expectantly for a familiar face among the mass of excited people around her. She kept her expression relatively composed when she realized she was more alone than she'd ever been. But as far as any *Taken*-style sex-trafficking kidnapper looming around was concerned, Ana was not a tourist.

It was the blistering summer that her parents both started new jobs and her sisters were infested with all-consuming boyfriends. Ana found she had nothing and no one, apart from a shitty minimum wage job at Burger Shack and the pale blue house with the red 1989 Ford F-150 truck in Hidalpa that was her birthright. So, she left with no return ticket.

She split her time between meals at the blue house and video games at Zahaira's house. After winning ten runs of *Mario Kart*, Zahaira made Ana promise she'd learn to drive so that she would finally be a worthy opponent.

All her life, the thing Ana had wanted more than anything was to sit in the front seat of her grandfather's truck and fly the wheels across fine beach sand. Her parents back home were useless, hardly ever needing a car in New York. With her Tío Christian as a teacher in Hidalpa, she'd be safely on the road—but maybe not before she was thirty. And Zahaira was only slightly better (at the very least, marginally louder).

"Did you really have to take me to a mountain for driving lessons? This seems like a level ten and I'm more at a level two," Ana complained. She felt the engine shaking below her every time they passed over a pebble. It felt like she was on an old roller coaster. The mountain was hardly paved, and if she looked to her right for too long, she could see the bare, unguarded cliff she easily imagined driving off of.

"Hey, if you can drive here, you can drive anywhere. Watch out! Coño!" Zahaira pointed out a hole ahead of them just before being thrashed against the roof of the car. Ana was still figuring out the mechanics of braking.

"Oops."

They'd seen nothing but goats and stray horses for miles.

"Shouldn't we be heading back soon?" Ana wondered. "Or are you planning on murdering me out here?" The crickets and frogs had begun stirring up their evening symphony.

"We're almost there."

The truck turned a corner onto a viewpoint enclosed by a low marble railing. They could see several towns below and the formation of curved land hugging the shore. Ana abruptly parked the car sideways near a herd of motorcycles. She could hear the merengue getting louder as she got out and gleefully ran to the edge. Zahaira trailed behind, satisfied with herself.

Girls were straddled over motorcycles. Plastic cups with glowing amber liquid appeared from an unknown source. The sun faded away and a circle cleared for dancing. Ana perched herself on top of the marble railing, tapping her foot to the beat. Zahaira leaned forward next to her. The cool mountain air was delicious.

They were in the middle of fake-arguing over which character was the best to play Mario Kart with when Ana first noticed the man with the machete. He was bothering another group of girls about something, clearly drunk. He was a jolly drunk, who occasionally slipped into a dance, though the absent- minded manner in which he held his machete, like a loose cigarette, made Ana's jaw tense. Zahaira had her back turned to him. Ana had seen much worse on the subway, but her intuition told her to stand up after she saw him staring at her friend's generous backside.

He had only begun approaching, hands eagerly outstretched, when she stopped him.

"Vete pa' otro la'o, viejito," Ana hissed, stepping defiantly between the man and Zahaira. Her small hands were wound into tight fists.

Zahaira turned around in disbelief. She put a hand on Ana's immovable shoulder. Then, she greeted the man gently and asked if he was looking for something. The man slurred his words, scraping his machete carelessly across the ground. Ana thought she heard him ask for a sip of her beer, and was seconds away from throwing her bottle at his head. Zahaira's hand pleaded Ana back. Her friend slipped a couple bills out of her pocket and pointed the man in the direction of a woman handing out beers from a cooler. The man turned around and terrorized another group on his way to the cooler.

Zahaira's shoulders released their tension. She pinched Ana's arms, leading them back to the truck.

"That was stupid. Don't ever do that again," Zahaira warned. "You're not my boyfriend."

That was the last thing Ana would remember her friend saying to her when she tried to fall asleep on her sister's couch years later. After a shaved head and retracted scholarship to NYU, her father's sponsored plane tickets would come to an end. And in their place was the ocean between them. It was an ocean Ana could only float on top of in peace, rather than dive into deep, murky waters. That was how she liked it.

* * *

The two girls stood in silence, watching rolls of seafoam creep over their toes. The sky was shifting its gradient every millisecond. Ana thought of a story she remembered reading in high school about a woman walking into the ocean because she was unhappy with her husband and children. She thought of the perseverance required to continue walking deeper and deeper against the weight of the ocean, and the uncertainty ahead. The landscape in front of her didn't seem any more real than a world without her abuela's rice waiting for her at home. She decided she would rather go out like her abuelo — in her sleep. Maybe sans the Alzheimer's and chest pain. It was rare that she went this long without rambling unfiltered thoughts onto the nearest victim.

"Should I be worried? Or is it just your usual dumbass-ery?" Zahaira offered trepidly. To her relief, Ana smiled.

"Usual dumbass-ery. Thinking about a story I read."

"Huh. I didn't know college dropouts could read."

"I hate you." Ana kicked Zahaira's leg. Her friend was laughing hysterically at her own joke. "Not even that funny. Rude."

"You could never hate me, you love me."

"You know what? You're right."

Zahaira stopped laughing as Ana regarded her. Ana reached forward and slipped the sunglasses off Zahaira's face and clipped them into her T-shirt. The fading sunlight shimmered off Zahaira's like a velvet rose. Ana had to remind herself to breathe.

"Ana . . ."

"Zahaira . . ." Ana whispered, mocking. She brushed her shoulder against Zahaira's. "Remember when we were eight and we used to 'run into each other' again and again one summer?"

"No," Zahaira lied. She didn't like where this was going.

"Well, I remember. I remember wishing I had your long hair. And your waist." Ana let her index finger graze Zahaira's cheek. "And your nails." Zahaira refused to meet her eyes. Ana took up Zahaira's right hand and thumbed over the crackled, white nail polish that popped brilliantly against her skin.

"My nails are so ugly," Zahaira mumbled. Ana shook her head.

"I hate people who can't take a compliment." She held Zahaira's hand hostage.

"And I can't stand liars," Zahaira countered.

"Said the liar."

"No me venga con esa vaina. I never lie. I just don't go around telling everyone all my business."

". . . Like I do, you mean?"

Ana's hand felt hotter than the sun. Zahaira brought herself to look at her, nose flared. She had no response. So, Ana steamrolled on.

"Do you like me?"

"Ana, how many times . . . of course I—"

"Do you like me? Even a little? Can you say that much?" Ana tried her best to keep traces of cruelty out of her mouth.

"I like you. You're my friend, Ana. We've done this already. I don't know what you want to hear."

Ana nodded slowly. She looked down and tightly interlocked her fingers with Zahaira's, meeting little resistance. She took a breath in before looking up into her partner's deep-brown eyes.

"Zahaira Marileidy DeLeón . . . I love you. I'm in love

with you. Absolutely everything about you. I'm saying it. You're hearing it. And I'm not taking it back because it's been true most of my life and it will never not be true. I don't care what you can or can't say." Ana let go of the air inside her, feeling lighter already. Zahaira quickly blinked away tears. She'd cried enough that day.

"I can't do this, Ana."

"Why not?"

"You're my best friend, stupid. That should be enough reason. And besides . . ." Zahaira reclaimed ownership of her hand and picked up another stone from the shallow water around them. She pictured the empty Belén house that had once beckoned Ana home. "You're gonna leave. You always do." She whipped the rock across the ocean, watching it skip into twilight. The sun's last tendrils of green were still holding on to the horizon.

1, 2, 3, 4, 5 . . .

Ana slipped a fresh stone into Zahaira's trembling hand, insistent.

"And what if I stay?"

IX.
Life After the Storm

The morning after the phone call from his Tío Gabriel came, Jorge was woken up and sent to the dry cleaner's on 167th Street where his mother got a 15% discount with a jar of her homemade sofrito. He'd groaned and only imagined his complaint before his mother stopped him with her classic hit, "When I was your age, I walked for miles—"

He decided to sing along with the familiar tune.

"—and miles, and miles. So many miles. Every morning to get water and you carried a goat on your back and did a marathon and didn't complain once, we get it." Jorge rolled his eyes as he raised himself from the mattress on the floor that was his bed. His mother pulled his ear in annoyance.

"Don't be a smartass. Criminals don't get to be smartasses." She turned towards the kitchen as he pulled his pillow over his head. "E'te muchacho es un castigo. I don't know what God wants me to do with you, Dios mío."

He tightened at the hardness growing in her voice. After she returned to the kitchen, two pans rang against each other and a drawer slammed. If he wasn't careful, Mami could go months without speaking to him. He was surprised she'd spoken to him at all that morning. But they'd been each other's only family for the past eight years, and he supposed she couldn't afford to lose him either. Not even over this. Especially not on a day when they were expecting company.

It wasn't his fault. Not really. Hustling just came too naturally to Jorge, even at his young age. He often felt like he must be the only one who saw all the cracks and seams and cheat codes throughout the city. And with so many lucrative possibilities that inflicted absolutely no harm to anyone. Except maybe tourists. And yet here he was — a fall man for his own business empire, taken out the game by a goddamn snitch. Eight boxes of the limited edition Jordan 8s he was moving thrown into the garbage chute by the Dean at St. Phillip's Academy, bringing his net worth back to zero. He'd hardly left his bed since. Today would mark ten days since he'd been expelled and his mother still hadn't found a school that would take him. He was waiting for her to finally accept that he belonged with the public school kids down the street — the ones she and her church friends feared when they saw them on the news every other month.

Jorge pushed the pillow off of his face. By now, Mami had turned on the radio and the voices of loud Dominicans arguing over island politics echoed into his room. If he closed his eyes and factored in the soft horns from the music playing at his neighbors', he could almost feel a warm breeze blowing through the window. Sometimes Jorge wondered why they ever left.

* * *

The dry cleaning lady took the homemade sofrito happily and sent Jorge off with good wishes to his mother. He wondered what the hell Mami and Mrs. Cho talked about when she came here. Neither of them speaking more than twenty words of English. Yet, Mrs. Cho looked at him as though she knew everything about his life.

"Be good," she told him. He could tell she really meant it, too.

Clutching a zipped black bag containing a thick leather coat, Jorge made his way back up Prospect. The coat had belonged to his father, back when he and Mami were having a thing two years ago. It didn't last long, but his father didn't have room in his suitcase for a winter coat, so it stayed. Mrs. Cho had managed to get the smell of Backwoods out of it, which was good because Jorge hated the smell of Backwoods. It had been sitting in the back of their closet infecting all the other jackets and scarves with its musty odor. Now it was like a new coat, free to live a new life.

Somewhere along Westchester and 163rd the freakin' snow started floating through the streets, teasing New York with its fleeting beauty. If Jorge were in school right now, he would probably be in Mr. White's Biology class. Probably staring out the window. Probably whispering to his classmates about what he was doing with the extra time from a half day. It was that kind of half-day snow. The heavy, sticky kind. He gave it an hour or two, tops, before the whole city was covered in piss-colored slush. But before Jorge knew it, the stupid fluff had him standing in the middle of the street, staring at the air around him. Like an idiot.

The first thing Jorge noticed was that the cop was tall — at least six foot three — with ginger hair poking out of his NYPD beanie. It was a wonder how Jorge hadn't seen him coming a mile away. He hadn't heard the cop at first when he asked Jorge what his name was. The second time he asked, he also reached for the dry cleaning bag, causing Jorge to flinch backward into a fighting stance. Idiot.

Now Jorge's heart was in his throat.

"Calm down, son. You speak English? Ha-blah English, huh?" Jorge wondered why Americans always spoke louder to non-English speakers?

" . . . Yeah. Sorry, is there something wrong, sir?" he finally said. Where the fuck did "sir" come from? Jorge's jaw tensed along with his grip on the bag. The cop narrowed his eyes. Jorge wondered, briefly, if he had anything incriminating on him. Or if it would even matter if the cop was matching him to a description. He usually wore his accent with pride, but at this moment, he regretted not paying more attention in ESL classes. The cop's tone made him feel like an unwanted weed being pulled from concrete.

"Whaddya have in that bag there?" The cop brought his hands to his waist.

Jorge couldn't help rolling his eyes. He was a businessman, not a petty thief. He brushed away the insult and slowly unzipped the dry cleaning bag to reveal the leather coat.

"Just picking up dry cleaning," Jorge hoped this would be the end of this interaction.

"Jeez, that's a nice coat. That your coat?" The cop reached to touch the leather, then rummaged his thick hands through the coat pockets. Jorge thought his jaw might pop out of his skull.

"No," he said calmly. "It's my father's, I'm just taking it home."

The cop pulled out what must've been the dry

cleaning receipt and tossed it on the snowy ground
haphazardly.

"And your name?"

"Jorge."

"Nice to meet you Jorge. Have a nice day and, uh, be
careful out here." He was smiling now, which made Jorge
feel like he had to smile back. The cop turned to his car.
Finally. Jorge let out the sharp, cold air that had built in
his lungs. His face was hot and the snow felt like it was
laughing at him, stinging his nose. He'd heard of things
happening to boys in his neighborhood — afterwards
they'd disappear or get into fights more, but it was like the
rumbling of the train, or his neighbors playing reggaeton
at 4:00 a.m. A disruption he'd grown accustomed to. One
he'd never been a part of before. Until now.

He knelt down to pick up the receipt and saw that
it was wrapped around a thin bracelet. Jorge looked up,
seeing that the cop car had driven away. He examined
the bracelet closer. It was a rosary bracelet — pale pink
and blue, made of intricately woven threads. Jorge ran
his fingers across the tiny braided cross at the end of it,
as though it were a talisman. He wondered if it belonged

to his father, but he'd never seen his father step foot in a church before. Then again, he hadn't seen his father do a lot of things.

Jorge put the bracelet in his pocket and composed himself. He looked up at the grey sky to God, or the universe, or whatever was out there. He asked a question he was asking himself a lot lately. Why? Why was he here? Why was he in this country, in this city, in this borough, in this life? Why wasn't he sitting on a beach eating a mango? Why did everyone — his mother, his school, that ginger cop — why did everyone think he was a criminal? Why did things like this keep happening to him? Why him? He waited for an answer that never came. Then, like a true New Yorker, he kept it moving.

* * *

"My mother used to say that her jewelry held memories. 'Like rocks in a river scarring with every wave,' I never knew what she meant," Tío Gabriel said as he tried on his new leather coat.

Gabriel was standing beside the only chair in their apartment (apart from the couch).

"Can I ask, is the United States always this cold?" his tío asked. He wanted to tell his strange uncle that yes, it was always bitterly cold except when it was suffocatingly hot.

"No," Jorge laughed. "Only New York, and only 'cause it knew you were coming, Tío,"

Jorge had met his tío for the first time moments ago. He was used to helping his mother host relatives and "old friends" he'd never met. Even though they lived in a one-bedroom apartment, his mother insisted they pass on the same hospitality they'd been shown so many years ago. When Jorge arrived back from the dry cleaners, Tío Gabriel was standing in the living room, reading a newspaper. Jorge almost karate-kicked him, thinking he was a robber who'd broken in. Apparently, his mother had told him where the spare key was hidden, in case he needed it. That didn't make his first impression of his uncle any less eerie. Outside of his rides on the A train, Jorge had never seen anyone read standing up. Tío Gabriel was wearing his hair in a short afro, with a patterned shirt and acid-wash jeans that belonged in another era. He was younger than Jorge had imagined him. After a big hug and formalities, Jorge handed him the jacket and showed him the woven bracelet.

"I think it's a rosario, like for praying. Wonder how long it was in there. But, I don't think it belonged to my papa, right?" Jorge said, twisting the bracelet around his fingers as he stood before his now seated uncle. He hated calling his father his papa; it felt so forced.

"I don't know. Let me see it," Gabriel motioned.

As Jorge slipped the bracelet into his tío's hand, he felt a bit of static run through his fingertips. He shook the feeling off.

"I think—" Gabriel stopped when the hallway light and the space heater simultaneously shut off. Luckily, they still had daylight coming through the window.

"¡Se fue la luz!" exclaimed Jorge. He quickly leaned into the circuit breaker in the hallway and flipped a switch to turn the heater back on. The hallway light stayed off. "Don't worry, our landlord's comin' tomorrow to fix the bathroom sink, anyways. He'll just have to add this to the list. This happens all the time. Anyways, is it my papa's or nah?"

"I think it was my Tía Lupe's. Your abuela. She was lovely, you would've liked her. A great singer. I'm pretty sure this belonged to her. My abuela would make ones just like these in her kitchen and Tía Lupe would sell them for her at the church. She was the head of the church in Hidalpa, you know?"

Jorge was stunned. He had never met his grandmother. She died when he was a toddler. His father never talked about her either — Jorge had never heard anything about her. He didn't even know her name until now. He wondered briefly why her bracelet was here, before realizing it might hold sentimental value. But his father didn't seem the sentimental type either.

Tío Gabriel twiddled with the bracelet for a moment longer before setting it on the table and sliding it back in Jorge's direction.

"Bueno, I think this belongs to you now," he said with finality. As Jorge regarded his tío, he realized that he had a couple hours to kill before his mother returned from work, and that the man was basically a walking family history book. He had a lot of questions to ask him and literally nothing to do and nowhere to go. Maybe this day didn't have to completely suck.

"I'll be right back. There's beer in the fridge, help yourself." Jorge grabbed the bracelet from the table before turning to go to the bathroom.

* * *

As soon as the bathroom door closed behind Jorge, his ears started ringing. It was getting louder and louder. His legs started to feel like lead. He turned to look at himself in the mirror and saw he was staring back with his hands pressed over his ears. In his reflection he saw water slowly rising up his neck, steadily rushing higher towards his chin. Yet, he saw no water around him on the black-and-white tile floor.

"What the fuck?"

He could feel the invisible water on his skin as he moved his arms. The bracelet had tied itself around his wrist somehow. Jorge suddenly felt himself choking on salt water and his toes floating off the ground. The scene in his reflection showed the water at ear-level now. He propelled his legs up through the invisible bathroom sea, took a deep breath, closed his eyes, and dove down with a splash.

As Jorge submerged, he felt a shift. The world turned over him like a carnival ride. He couldn't feel the floor at all. When he opened his eyes, he was alone in a bright, twinkling ocean, with the black-and-white bathroom tiles far above him. Below him, a rotting, sunken ship and black abyss. He swam to the surface for air, terrified, reaching for the familiar bathroom floor.

When Jorge broke free at the surface, he spat out at least a pint of water, catching his breath. He found himself not in an ocean, but a river. The sun was beating down on him, instantly warming his skin. He felt cold stones below him, his toes gripping for stability against violent waves. He found his hands wrapped around a tree branch. His body was different, but he noticed their wrist still adorned with the pink-and-blue bracelet. In the distance, there were dark-skinned women dressed in white, washing clothes on the rocks. They were staring in his direction, distracted from the laundry.

He looked down and saw that he was also wearing a white dress and that he was . . . different. There were long strands of coarse, black curls plastered all over his face, blocking his vision.

"Consuela! Consuela!" The women were shouting after him — her. He was Consuela now. And somehow he felt he knew her, or that he'd known her somehow. Consuela took over his motor functions. She took them to the women, still struggling to breathe as they waded against the current.

"¡Gracias a Dios! ¿Y Maria?" One woman grabbed them up by their arm. Her Spanish had an accent. She sounded like Jean-Paul, Jorge's first friend at St. Phillips Academy. Haitian, he realized. She shook their shoulders urgently. "¡Maria! ¿Y Maria?" Jorge felt the tears streaming down their already-wet face. The shouting woman manically rushed herself down the river, white dress trailing behind. Their tears kept coming and coming. When the other woman pulled them in for a hug, they let out a scream into her chest. He'd never felt anything like this before. It was a guttural pain. Her tears were mixed with his, too. They were intertwined. He felt how young

Consuela was — maybe ten or twelve at most. He knew
that Maria was around the same age. He knew who Maria
had been. And he knew Maria couldn't swim.

They felt even more water dripping down their
cheeks, at first believing it was coming from the waves
or that they were imagining it. They looked above them,
Jorge for the second time that day (if this even was the
same day? Or was he dreaming?). The sky looked like a
scene from the Bible. Lightning, grey clouds, basically
a Renaissance painting. The ceremonious sky parted
and dumped a flood of rain onto them. They closed their
eyes and stuck out their tongue to taste the rain. In this
moment of painful grief, briefly, there is hope. I am
Consuela. I will live.

* * *

When he opened his eyes again, he was in the dark.
Definitely not the same day. The rain had stopped, but he
was still wet. This time his legs were wet and his skirt —
her skirt? — was dragging below him as he wrung out a
towel. He was new now. He stopped wringing the towel

and turned to look at a mirror. He could tell they were
kind of pretty, even in the shadows.

Lupe.
The name was beamed into his head.

Wait, Lupe? He looked down. Still there — distinctly
pink and blue even in the darkness. The bracelet. Abuela
Lupe's bracelet? Their bracelet. This was a lot. They went
back into auto-mode, with Lupe taking control. They were
nearly hysterical. He could feel their heartbeat flying. There
was water rising below them in this tiny wooden room,
with several leaks in the aluminum roof. Why did water
keep trying to kill him? They were wading through the
flood carrying buckets and towels and candles back and
forth. Along with the sounds of what must be a hurricane
throwing around trees outside, inside rang the sound of a
pregnant woman letting out short bursts of terrifying cries.

They were Lupe. No one else was around. Just them
and the pregnant woman. No one to save them but Lupe
and a pregnant woman. A pregnant woman who was
definitely mid-birth, by the looks of it. Her legs were

spread and raised on the bed she was perched atop of. A bed that was rising steadily with the water level approaching the edges of the mattress.

"Cálmate, Mabel. Cálmate." They found themselves reassuring the pregnant woman who was also their sister. Jorge marveled at how calm they were. He would have been freaking out. He was freaking out. But Lupe seemed to be calming him as well. Still, they needed help. Through the open doorway, they had just seen a wall in the kitchen collapse. And pretty soon they would be floating up to this shoddy ceiling to drown if they couldn't find a way out to higher ground. Mabel yelled again, this time in sync with a crack of thunder (Tía Abuela Mabel, Jorge reminded himself.) They could see the baby's head between her legs now. He was no nurse, but Jorge instinctively knew this was a bad sign. It was not far along enough for the timeline this flood had in mind.

As if things couldn't get any worse, the only doorway in this room was now blocked by another obstacle — the kitchen stove on the other side had burst into flames. Jorge was genuinely scared now, but Lupe was not. Lupe had her God and she was not dying today.

Mabel let out another yell in sync with the thunder. Something was seriously off about her.

They swam over to a floating metal box and grabbed it over their head. Looking up at the dimly lit ceiling, they found a large hole in the roof with a patch of rust around it. The storm was leaking through. With their right arm, they knocked the corner of the box into the rust. To Jorge's surprise, they made a sizable dent. God, how many weights was his abuela lifting? After three more hits, they pierced through one side. They tried again on the other side, chaos still swirling around them. Another big chunk shattered above them, revealing a sky of dimly lit stars through the clouds. They brushed the rust and dirt off their face and assessed the situation again.

The bed frame was now floating in the water, puddles forming on the mattress. Lupe threw a wet towel over her shoulder and went to Mabel's side. They pushed the bed frame with a bit of strength and it glided two inches away.

"Vamos," they decided. "Al techo. Vamos Mabel, tenemos que salir de aquí. Tu tienes que salir de aquí. Por Gabriel. Yo te levantare. Vamos." There was no hesitation or tremor in their gruff, authoritative voice as they persuaded Mabel to get up. Gabriel is coming, Jorge realized. Tío Gabriel.

"No, no puedo. Vete tu, Lupe. No puedo," Mabel cried out between strained breaths. Lupe moved forward. She went to the other side of the bed, and, using the wall for leverage, pushed the bed beneath the hole they'd made in the ceiling. Jorge felt his strength intertwine with his abuela's. They made it. Next step, they climbed on top of the mattress, sitting beside their sister.

"Vamos," they repeated, looking deep in Mabel's eyes. They turned their back to the woman and pulled her arms over their shoulders. "Agárrate." Mabel obeyed and tightened her grip. They tucked Mabel's legs under their arms and slowly stood up. Mabel's head made it through the hole. Now what? They sat back down and told Mabel to stand. Mabel obeyed again. They could feel her legs shaking. "Un . . . dos . . . tres." Jorge felt himself expand. They felt every muscle radiating pain. Mabel pushed down, crushing their shoulders, and lifted herself up from their foundation. And she was gone. She was alive.

Alive and on the roof with her son. They heard her let

out a guttural scream. It sent a shiver down their spine. If this baby came out healthy, it would be a miracle.

After a beat, the rain thinned out. A hand popped down from the roof.

"No," they said, to Jorge's surprise. They thought of the baby, of the already difficult pregnancy. They couldn't risk any more damage.

"¡Vamos!" yelled the voice from above. "Vamos, Lupe."

They stared at the hand. Take it! Jorge pleaded. They grabbed the metal box again and stood on it. They still had a way to go. Lupe gave in and let herself be pulled through the ceiling. They could see the stars shimmering brighter above them. Jorge felt himself rise to his place among the constellations.

* * *

And then Jorge was on a tile floor again. This time a dirty one. But he still wasn't Jorge. He was starting to feel like someone was playing a prank on him. His head felt hazy and his stomach was turning. Jorge pulled themself up, wondering how much longer this would go on. They were

a woman again, he could feel it. They held a bracelet-clad
hand onto a nearby sink for stability, and he was shaken
by their reflection in the cloudy mirror in front of them.
They wiped some vomit off of their mouth and tucked
their hair behind their ears. Jorge looked into the eyes he'd
known his entire life.

"Luciana Jimenez!"

They heard their name being called, a name Jorge
knew she had been waiting all day for. His mother's name.

"Luciana Jimenez!" They scrambled out of the
bathroom facility with their snakeskin purse and returned
outside to their place in line. A stout woman with a
baby had been holding it for them. They raised their
hand and affirmed they were present for their 7:00 a.m.
appointment at the US Consular Section. The sun was
beating like it was 1:00 p.m., though.

"Esta línea," the officer pointed to the shorter line
of people next to where they were standing. They walked
over and addressed the same officer.

"Mi nombre es Luciana Jimenez. Soy la hija de Lupe—"

"E'perate," the officer cut her off and gruffly grabbed
her purse, riffling through the papers inside and patting

her down. Jorge wasn't a fan of how long his hands lingered on her ass.

When he was finished he just walked away, disappearing behind the single red door in front of them. They stood stupefied by the man's abruptness. The stout older woman in front of them explained that there was a person inside that would ask the questions and make the approval. She reminded them of Lupe, as she went on about how her son got a job in Miami and had requested her for a green card. This was the special line for the requested people, she explained, and they handed out green cards fast to people like them. She went on for at least five more minutes. Luciana zoned out and covered their eyes from the relentless sun. They tried to remember that they were lucky. That people had it much worse than them. That pregnant women were drowning in boats and crossing deserts to do what she only had to bring a form to a building to do.

Mi nombre es Luciana Jimenez. Soy la hija de Lupe Jimenez. Ella me pidió una tarjeta de residencia. Ella es mi madre y ha sido ciudadana estadounidense durante cinco años,

viviendo en Nueva York. Aquí están mis papeles. Mi nombre es
Luciana . . .

They went over the script they'd written over and
over, mouthing the words. Jorge knew they were lies.
They were not the daughter of Lupe Jimenez. Lupe was
his father's mother, not Luciana's. He knew now that
Lupe had moved to New York and became a citizen. He
stretched himself, bursting with questions, and Luciana
glided her hands over her stomach. Her expression
changed from strained to focused. He felt like she was
tossing her thoughts at him, like when they were at
St.James Park playing handball in the summertime.

His grandmother, Lupe, had married a Dominican-
American man after her retirement and moved to New
York. She loved absolutely everything from the food to
the subway to the Ghanaian Jehovah's Witnesses who
constantly appeared at her door. Luciana still talked to
Lupe all the time, despite her separation from Tito. It
didn't matter that they were no longer bound by Lupe's
meandering son. They were family. Now even more so,
since Lupe was the only one who knew her secret. And

when Luciana told her she'd lost her job at the hat factory, Lupe didn't hesitate to invite her to the States. All she had to do was lie — barely lie. Lupe was basically her mother in all the ways that counted.

Mi nombre es Luciana Jimenez . . .

They went back to their reciting, like a robot returning to factory settings. The sun was becoming unbearable at this point. They wished a street vendor would come around with water or coconuts or, really, anything. Mangoes! She loved mangoes. If her mouth weren't so dry, it would be watering. They were too close to the door now to risk jumping off line again. Plus, they were certain that a physical check-up was waiting for them on the other side. As much as they loved mangoes or coconuts, they never knew what might send their stomach back to the bathroom.

Jorge could feel the splitting headache returning. Their legs were starting to feel like spaghetti as they moved up the line. This was not a good time. Once Jorge had the thought, the sky immediately turned grey and a flash of dry lightning danced across the air.

Water.

It came down gently, baptizing their forehead with the coldest water in the world it seemed. They breathed in and out slowly, before thanking God for his grace, and returning to their script.

Mi nombre es—

"Luciana Jimenez?" A blonde woman with a clipboard peeked behind the door. They realized they'd reached the front of the line. They grabbed the envelope out of their bag, took a deep breath, and followed the woman through the red door. It closed behind them with a

Snap.

Gabriel's hands were suddenly in front of his face. He snapped his fingers again.

"Are you here?" Tío Gabriel's eyes were examining him intently, inches away from Jorge's own. "Are you okay, hijo?"

Jorge felt as if his bones had been torn apart and mashed back together. He could feel every muscle and ligament and blood vessel in his body. They were all arguing with one another, shouting over one another, speaking different languages. He twitched a pinky up and it felt like he was uprooting a skyscraper. He straddled gratitude, grief, anger, loneliness, defiance — it was too much for him to contain. Despite his state, he slowly realized that he was standing in the middle of his living room. Everything was just as he'd left it.

He ran his hands over his arms and chest, bewildered by his own existence. It was his body. His body. A male one. Not a drop of water was on it. He touched his cheeks, where streams of silent tears were turning to salt. The sunlight was still beaming through the window. A soft hum of cars brought him back to earth.

"I . . . I was . . . I-I . . . ." Jorge struggled to find words.

His uncle urgently grabbed his wrist with gentle force. Jorge felt the rosary burning through his skin. Gabriel pulled it off of him and threw the bracelet into the kitchen sink. He took Jorge by the shoulders and sat him

down in the only chair in the room. His Tio grabbed him
by the chin.

"You are okay." Tío Gabriel asserted sternly. "You will
be okay. But you need to eat, papi." He handed Jorge a box
of saltine crackers. Jorge wasn't sure whether he would
be okay. As much as logic was pulling his brain, insisting
he'd had a harmless daydream, Jorge felt his past spirits
cementing themselves within him, forming community.
He would never be okay again. He could never be just
him — singular. His body belonged to them.

X.
Domino

Most days that year after a starch-heavy supper, along with the children and the elderly, a teenage Aribel could be dependably found sharing a bed with her pregnant Tía for an afternoon nap. She savored these naps. The midday air would settle into beads of sweat on her caramel skin as a dusty plastic fan blew salt crystals onto her back. And she would wake up clammy and delirious, somewhere outside of time and space, until her mother shouting disbelief at her daughter's laziness would tune the girl's ears into focus. And the sun would bleed into the next day's siesta hour. So the time warp of summer continued.

But one day near the end of August, after a thunderstorm shook out all the dust the night before, the air had peculiarly dried out and the leftover winds brought a delicious relief. Her legs became restless reaching for a glimpse of this rare afternoon. So, Ari tossed the scraps of her meal to the neighbor's dog, dug her volleyball out from under the bed, and detached the pair of Pumas hanging from the windowsill. How could anyone sleep when the ground was so cool and the smell of fallen rain so intoxicating? It was the kind of weather that made her wish she was a track star, so she could run to the mountains and scream as she felt all her breath renew itself. Though she wasn't much of an athlete, she kissed her Pumas to the street and walked to her neighbor's door.

"How're we getting there, then?" She bumped the volleyball to Rafaela a little too low. Rafaela dove to save it. Ari took note to account for their height difference.

"One of the guaguas, I guess. El hijo de Martin told me yesterday that the little ones leave for the capital every two hours starting at six." Rafaela's long, skinny, brown legs lunged wherever the breeze blew Ari's wild hits. Still, she was never out of breath. Ari, on the other hand, had to find her balance after each hit. She set the ball back and scratched the braids pulling her scalp.

"Two hundred pesos?"

"Two hundred pesos. Each."

"You got four hundred pesos?" Ari pursed her lips.

"Nena, if Romeo Santos is gonna be there, I'll sweep all the hair in the world for my two hundred pesos," Rafaela laughed. "You better find your own. Maybe my mother'll pay you, too, if you come by the salón."

"Bro, I can't believe they're really coming to Santo Domingo next month. And for a free concert. Free. Why doesn't nobody ever come here?"

Rafaela laughed again and shook her head at her neighbor. In the middle of the street, in front of both their homes, the two had found their groove. Ari bumped high up. Rafa set it back down.

"How many people do you think'll be there?" Ari continued.

"Millones, chiqui. I hear that one song everywhere."

"Son las cinco de la mañana
y yo no he dormido nada."

Ari swung her thick hips into a bachata before hitting

the next bump. The two girls let out an unruly giggle as the ball leapt into the air. "¡Oye ! What if—"

Rafaela spun her head around and watched helplessly. "Jo-der . . ."

Behind her stood the towering brick wall that encircled the Díaz property. In spite of the mystery that surrounded the tiny, wooden main house and its two-house-long backyard, the girls knew that the walls contained at least one rooster, a smelly goat, a gaggle of toddlers, and now — one single volleyball.

Three lock clicks and the shuffling of heavy feet greeted Ari's politest knock. An aged and spotted hand cracked open the lopsided wooden door as wide as the final lock chain would allow. A glassy, green eye inspected them like they were trying to sell him something.

" . . . Saludos," Rafaela started. She elbowed her partner.

"Sí, saludos Don Díaz." Ari waited for a beat. The old man only let out a grunt. "Bueno, we're here for my ball — well my volleyball — it's just, it's in your . . . yard area."

"Perdónanos, señor," Rafaela apologized preemptively

before the man could get a word in. He shifted his
eyes between the two girls cautiously. Then, the door
slammed shut. Ari fought her hand from forming a fist
and smashing a hole into the house, but just as she shifted
her weight backward, the door swung again and a
black cane struck down to prop it open.

"What is it?" This brief and simple snap revealed the
old man's deeply southern accent.

"Sorry. My ball, it's—"

"We don't have it." Period.

"But—"

"Junior!" He shouted over his shoulder. "You seen
a volleyball?" (Junior shook his head.) "We don't have it.
Buen día." Junior was sitting on the dirt floor scraping
a styrofoam plate of food. Behind him, Ari watched a
diapered toddler running after a white ball in the yard
through the back entry. The blood rushed from her fists
to her ears as she watched the little gremlin kick her ball
against a pile of bricks. She turned her attention back to
crusty old Don Díaz, meeting his eyes in a stalemate. It
was she who eventually conceded and turned back the
same way she came. She knew he was done talking. Any

more words she exchanged were above her quota for respectability as a teenager speaking to an ancestor.

* * *

Two weeks later, Ari and Rafaela emerged from Colmado Belén with the day's groceries, giggling as they continued plotting their scheme to get to the upcoming Aventura concert. A man with a stack of plastic lawn chairs nearly knocked over Ari's perfectly fluffed afro. She turned to ask her grandfather, Don Belén, who was smoking his afternoon cigar at the counter, what was going on with the chairs. They were setting up for a dominoes tournament, he told her. And it was the big leagues. Ari watched as a particularly wretched old man crawled his way down the street using his house chair as a makeshift cane. He dragged his plastic faded green chair up to the fold-out dominoes table and took a labored descent into his seat.

Rafaela shot Ari a look. She could see Ari's mind was already in another place. On occasion, she'd found it was exhausting being her friend.

"How do I sign up?" Ari set down her groceries.

Her grandfather smiled through his cigar smoke.
"My flesh and soul, it's seventy-five pesos to sign up, and
six hundred pesos to the winner. Starts in five minutes."
He spoke sweetly and reached behind his dusty case of
trophies to hand over a clipboard.

"Ari, no," Rafaela whined. They'd worked every day
for two weeks to raise what little money they had. Not to
mention, they hadn't factored in the cost of food or cab
fares once they arrived in the capital.

"Ari, sí. And Rafa, too. Put your bags down and pull
up a chair, flaca."

* * *

Ever since Jesus had risen, the stone benches beneath the
town's immense tamarind tree hosted the same rotation
of elderly uncles and their middle-aged nephews. The
sound of shuffling ivory — echoing especially far on
Saturday evenings — rivaled the sound of the old bones
that shifted themselves to get there. Despite crass insults
about mothers and daughters and whores being tossed
across the board, a little girl with her hair bound in

signature twin puffs had felt no qualms about enjoying her Blow Pop at her grandfather's lap.

At age three, Ari learned to dance bachata and merengue by stepping on her father's feet. By similar process, at age five she learned to cook rice by sitting on the kitchen counter between her mother and aunt, and at age six she absorbed her grandfather's gaming moves serving as his harmless lap accessory beneath the tamarind tree. She would sit in silence, observing every slammed piece, counting the board, and trying her best to keep up. The funnest games always involved her great uncles battling each other in wits. To a young Ari, it seemed dominoes was a game of mind-reading, mixed with quick math and fortune-telling. After one prosperous afternoon, Ari carried home her grandfather's miniature trophy and berated him with questions. Like how did he know that the tío on his left had the double-six piece? Don Belén confided in his granddaughter about the lizard that slid across the table and whispered advice in his ear. The lizards, the birds, the cats, and even the flies had a way of speaking to him, he'd said. With a dewy-eyed grin, Ari asked how old she'd be when she would talk to the animals, too. Before you know the animals, you have to know people, mi niña.

She never quite figured out the animals, but the summer Ari turned eleven, her investment in training Rafaela to read her mind and count dominoes at the expense of undone chores finally paid off. They spent the twenty-five pesos they won on the sweetest bagged ice cream they'd ever had and spent the rest of the year craving more.

* * *

Thankfully, the years had not diminished the magic of the girls' hustle. With two games under their belt, Ari sat beside her final opponent, grateful he had the skill to make it this far. His virulent green-eyed stare held the same empty arrogance of the string of old men that had come before him. It was like they were doing her a favor when they started playing, giving her some charity by allowing her to experience their priceless wisdom.

Usually, she felt sorry for them and the fragility of their world. Though this particular sip of elderly ego she was purely relishing.

"Here's what we're gonna do — you can keep the six hundred pesos right now . . ." Ari started, ceremoniously shuffling the white pieces with her palms like a magician. " . . . if you do me a favor and gift me a volleyball, señor."

Don Díaz gruffly ignored her and snatched up his seven game pieces. He slammed down a double six.

"Your turn."

Ari and Rafaela exchanged a look across the table. The old man's partner collected his pieces and they continued in strained silence. Ari only broke the tension twice by sucking her teeth and whispering curses when the old man blocked her turns. From the moment she had read her hand, she knew the only way to win was to set the game for Rafa's victory. She counted and recounted every second, mentally placing the unplayed pieces in each of the players' hands, and calculating future possibilities. The old man put down his 3-2 and Ari smiled, having seen her vision come true. He was playing for himself, not his partner.

Finally, Rafaela put down her second-to-last piece with telepathic counsel from Ari. Don Díaz took a long sip of his beer before he slammed down the one piece Ari was dreading, effectively locking his partner out of the game and leaving it in her hands. She'd mentally placed that one in Rafaela's hands at the beginning of the game. What a little shit.

"Coño," Rafaela sighed.

"Wait. Paciencia, señores . . . paciencia." Ari set down her hand facedown and retraced the game. One of them had the final 4 piece and one had the final 6, and Ari had both. If Rafaela had the piece she guessed, they would win — but if not . . .

Ari and Rafaela stared at each other for a full minute, exchanging different variations of eyebrow lifts and pursed lips. Don Díaz signaled his impatience with a cough.

"Okay," Ari settled.

"Okay. You got this," Rafaela echoed.

Ari flipped over her piece. The onlookers standing behind Rafaela let out a cheer. Rafa slammed down her final piece with vengeance, causing the board to levitate.

The old man sat still for a moment before throwing his piece down, pushing himself back and walking away stolidly. The circle of old and young men surrounding them broke into raucous laughter. Rafaela joined them and nearly took Ari down by jumping on top of her.

"Maldito viejo, ¡coño! ¡Dame mi quarto!" Rafa kissed her friend on the cheek, smiling brightly.

Still, Ari was pissed that she hadn't factored the old man's pride into the game. Her grandfather emerged from the colmado and gave his granddaughter a kiss on the cheek and a paperclip-bound six hundred pesos. As the sun dipped beyond the horizon and the air around them melted into pink, Rafaela perked up. She pointed behind Ari to a young shirtless boy dashing around the corner. He had dried tears salted on his face and a mud-covered volleyball straddled in his skinny arms.

The boy dropped the ball into Ari's hands and stuck out his own hand for a shake. "Con permiso," his voice like sandpaper. It was not much in terms of apologies.

She looked him over and turned to Rafaela, before tentatively taking the boy's hand. And that was it. He turned back the same way he came.

XI.
High Spirits

Nochebuena was a familiar ritual — spirits high, bubbling artificial smiles bursting through the room with every sip. This year, now ripened at age twelve, Gabriel was for the first time handed his very own bottle of Presidente, dressed in a white wedding gown and cumbersome in his hands. He attempted to act as though he were well-versed in the art of drinking alcohol. But it wasn't as if his cousins or parents paid him much attention. Their eyes were jolly and bright and always focused on the storyteller. Aunts and uncles each taking their turn, their tales passed down from the generations above them, offering a bridge between the young earth and the fossil stars. Similar gestures prevailed among Doña Mabel's sisters and even her brother as they individually preached to the group. But, it was the unquestionable truth that Doña Mabel crafted tales the most like their recently late mother, an authority on the storytelling medium. And so it was she who now had the floor.

Doña Mabel's choice tale for Nochebuena was always pious and about love, in honor of the holy day of Christ's birth. The story of her own love, or the miraculous births of her own children, usually. On the night that Gabriel sipped his first drink, though, it seemed that the air was different than the rest, and his mother spoke more freely than usual. Papa José Sr. was in a good way, as well. He sat beside La Doña, listening intently and pleased that his guests were pleased. To him, she was like a toy in a music box that kept spinning and spinning, so simple, and yet a marvelous acquisition, with impeccable memory.

On this occasion, the story went that Mabel was seventeen when she met José. She was a quiet but intelligent girl from Matanzas, still living with her family, while occasionally catching a freight train to the city to study nursing on merit. Her hair was a long and shining black crown atop her head (she always mentioned this nostalgically, always). The black strands flowed with the wind as she sat on the train to school every Friday, surrounded by bundles of raw sugarcane wrapped with knots of palm leaves. Every Friday she waved to the blurred shadow of a passing farm boy standing on the horizon. And so it happened that she was peeling potatoes with her sister in the kitchen one Thursday afternoon when a businesslike knock emerged from the front door. She shared a quizzical look with Norena, and with a rebellious smile, went to go open the door, despite the fact that her mother and father were not home.

"Señorita Jimenez?" Before her stood a tall young man dressed up in a soldier's costume that was just a half inch too long. His hair was slicked back and had a pleasing auburn glow against his toasted brown skin. A slim pencil mustache had formed of sheer willpower atop his lip. Sometimes she mentioned the pencil mustache, other times it was a matured beard, depending on José's temperament that day. This boyish soldier was a new face, which was rare in Matanzas.

"This is the Jimenez house. But which Señorita

Jimenez, sir? I am the second youngest, but maybe you'd want my older sister—" She retreated her head towards the dining room.

"No — well, no. I think, no. La Señorita Mabel Jimenez? That is you?" Mabel opened the door a bit wider and scrutinized the man before her. "My girl on the train? Yes, I can see now that it is you." He smiled devilishly.

Mabel felt a blush coming on. And at this point, La Doña would stop and wait for the giggles and awws from her audience. What a fairy tale, that's what her nieces at the Nochebuena table would say, marveling at the glazed, giddy look in her aged husband's eyes they would mistake for romance.

In her youth, the sensation of having been watched overwhelmed the young girl. She tried not to show it.

"I am Mabel," she asserted. "What can I help you with?"

"Um . . . Well, mi amor, if your father is home . . . perhaps that would make this easier?" He attempted to look past her, but she closed the door slightly.

"Afraid not, sir. Just us girls today. And my mother just left for the market. Maybe you can return tomorrow when he gets back? Or I can take a message, if that would please you?" She could see he was becoming uneasy.

"Well, you see, sugar, the thing is I'm going away in two days. By wish of the government. (He gestured towards his attire). Anyway, I came here for you." He paused to remove his cap. "I've spent the two days since I learned I was drafted trying to find out who you were. It's a long story, but I finally got to your family butcher, who told me where I might find you. And well, you don't know it yet, but I intend to marry you. So please pass on this note to your father, requesting your presence at my family's ranch in Hidalpa tomorrow at noon. I must be going back now, but I intend to see you soon." He stuck his hand out from his lengthy sleeves and offered a slip of parchment paper. After a quick bow of courtesy, he turned to leave.

"And did you see him soon?" a voice would pipe from somewhere in the adolescent section of the room. At times Doña Mabel felt compelled to say "No" with a chuckle and to muse on how different her life might have been.

"Of course," she smiled gingerly at her young, curly-haired niece. "My parents were ecstatic, naturally. The next day came, and your abuelito arranged a carriage to guide him and me to the ranch in Hidalpa." Mabelita's mother had lent her a dress from her wardrobe and a swipe of her lip rouge to increase her chances. La Doña sometimes mentioned that she wasn't at the time sure she wanted any chances to begin with. This would garner laughs from her youngest sister and eye rolls from her husband, if he was drinking rum.

When they arrived at the small, solitary ranch house amidst Hidalpa's sugarcane fields, another carriage with a white horse was also waiting at the door. Mabel's father, Don Cristobal, a proud military man and teacher, fixed the collar of his shirt and knocked on the door. After cordial welcomes between the Don and her suitor's mother, the stout, dark-skinned woman led them into the parlor. On her way down the brief corridor, she mentioned casually that she hoped her son would be able to choose between the two girls quickly. Due to his situation, of course.

The parlor opened up before them and a young, blue-eyed, brown-haired creature, no more than fifteen years of age, met her gaze timidly from the sofa. It was then that Mabel realized the situation life had thrown her into.

He was making up his mind, and she was being tested.
In the next room, the young José was sitting in the dining
room alone, scraping what was left of his meal. She took a
deep breath, thought of the lesson on herbal remedies she
was missing today, and decided with certitude that she
would fulfill her duty. (And of course, José wasn't too hard
to look at, La Doña would joke the year prior — though
she missed this relief point during tonight's retelling).

"Señor, por favor, the men are out back." Mabel
watched her father depart and suddenly she felt exposed.

The young, blue eyes from the sofa bounced
throughout the tension in the room, until finally the girl
stood up and introduced herself as Grimelda. She politely
bowed and excused herself from the room to go clean up
in the kitchen. Grimelda snuck the briefest expectant look
back towards the house matriarch for approval. José's
mother didn't seem too pleased. Mabel became aware that
everything she did from that point on was a part of the test.

"Siéntate," the older woman told Mabel.

Then came the cross-examination of questions. What
are your surnames? What does your father do? What
did your grandfather do? What are your measurements?

Do you have Spanish blood? Do you have Haitian blood? Beyond cooking, what are your skills? Can you read? Are you a virgin? (At this the littlest cousins would let out a giggle.) Are there any illnesses in your family?

José's mother seemed impressed that she was skilled in nursing. ("Very good . . . mmm . . . very good," La Doña would give her best impression of a stoic old woman.) Mabel tried her best not to look like a lost goat on the road. What were the fathers talking about? Was Don Cristobal haggling his daughter's worth or her suitor's? Mabel admitted she had little confidence in his ability to defend her. (Oops, may God bless his soul.) Eventually, Grimelda returned from her kitchen assignment and sat back down. She was instructed to wait as the old woman led Mabel to the kitchen.

"¿Como vamo?" she asked her son.

"Not bad. The beans were dry, though." José ignored Mabel as he addressed his mother. "Very pretty," he added. They continued assessing the girl in the next room.

Mabel looked around the kitchen, silently wondering what combination of herbs produced the effects of arsenic her professor had demonstrated a month prior. (A joke, of course. In actuality, she would say, she was speechless in the presence of his staggering confidence.) Finally, her wardens turned their attention to her. She was tasked with making José café con leche and a dessert. Then she would mop up the kitchen floor. Mabel looked briefly at her dear mother's dress and prayed it would survive the housework. The matriarch swiftly left the kitchen as soon as her instructions were through.

As she had learned to prepare when she was three, Mabel went to work on the café con leche, starting the fire on the stove. She ground the sugarcane, feeling the judging eyes of the soldier on her. She wondered if he had any knowledge of what she was doing. Her father had always made his own café, but her older brother could not even boil water. Like her mother had taught her, she added her sugar to the milk just as it was steaming, intoxicating the air with that familiar smell of breakfast.

For dessert, she took the leftover beans and concocted what would later be referred to throughout Hidalpa as her famous habichuelas con dulce, a sweet bean pudding. She waited patiently beside the table after serving José. Moments passed.

". . . Not dry." He shot a flash of the same wicked smile before returning to his habichuelas. She didn't find it as charming this time. "Mmm," was his critique of her café con leche.

Her years of house training kicking in, Mabel finished mopping the floor before the last drop of caffeine was drained from her suitor's cup.

"Done," José proclaimed, sliding out his plate. And with that single word, both their fates were sealed. The most delicious café con leche and habichuelas con dulce José would ever taste had prevailed and convinced him that Mabel was the one for him. This is where the story would usually end. On this Nochebuena, however, Doña Mabel continued.

"Done," José proclaimed, sliding out his plate. With this, she recalled her younger self collecting his finished cup of café and remembering her grandmother's practice of reading the coffee grinds left at the bottom of a cup, in order to predict the future. On childhood summer evenings, she would joke with her sisters and grandmother over more empty cups of coffee than any of them could drink, writing their destinies in the leftovers. So, she looked intently for what seemed like whole minutes (but what must have been seconds) into the depths of her future husband's empty cup. She didn't believe in superstitions, she would go on to say. Her only belief was in the Heavenly Father, Himself. Still, the knowledge that José's coffee-stained future was loosely linked to another soul, and that their journey was plagued with pain and discontent, along with a demon-ridden child — this was knowledge that would haunt her wedding day and each of her births. She shifted her gaze towards her youngest son, who was awkwardly cradling a beer in his hands. Gabriel's eyes met her's.

Doña Mabel smiled at her nieces and wondered aloud at her own silliness. She ended with something about her ongoing devotion to the Church, and the blessings it brought to her life regardless. With this abrupt new conclusion, Gabriel learned his mother could read coffee grinds, and that she was a good liar.